Mother of Wolves

Mother of Wolves

Evalyce – Worldshaper Book 1

J. Aislynn D' Merricksson

Published 2015 by Creativia
Book design by Creativia (www.creativia.org)
Cover art by http://www.thecovercollection.com/
Visit Port Jericho!
www.aislynndmerricksson.com
Visit our Facebook page!
www.facebook.com/Evalyce

This book is dedicated those who are my life-blood
and strong, loving support:

To Brother Wildfire and Mercurius Greyeyes, my deepest
inspirations.

To Jonas Merricksson, twice lucky one, my callowayla.

To Beth Finley, who inspired me to open the door to De Sikkari.

To Michael Calabrase, Goshen, my soul-mate and nemesis.

To Chris and Brandi Gore, anamcara and truest of friends.

To John and Sam Owens, my steady and strong support.

To Anish and Tania, who helped make this possible!

To my family of heart and soul,
To my blood-family and
To my bond-family-
There are far too many of you to name here! I love you all the
same, each and every one.

In loving memory of Nina Clark
who taught me my own Dance
and fostered in me a love of learning.

May the One who is All And Nothing
forever guide your steps. Nasmala!

Contents

Firefall

Isle of Whispers, Year of the White Boar, 2012 CE

Al'dhumarna yawned, stretching his essence, exploring the confines of his cage yet again. Something had awoken the Nagali from his ages-old slumber, something powerful and world-shattering. Whatever it was had weakened the binding the Magi of old had placed upon him, turning him to mythril.

With time, he would be free. All he had to do was wait. What were a few more years to one who had waited millennia for freedom? He would wait, oh yes. Wait and gather allies.

The great Nagali sent part of his essence out, questing for just the right kinds of sympathetic minds to aid him. Minds hungry for power, for wealth, for revenge. All these things he promised them, in exchange for their devotion and obedience. Sibilant instructions were given, plans laid by the trapped demi-deity against the time when he would finally be free again.

Unknown Location, Year of the Golden Hart, 2013 CE

A young man lay twitching and whimpering in his sleep, tormented by nightmares. A cool voice slid through his thoughts demanding obedience and promising swift punishment should it be lacking. The voice was not happy with his conduct of late. It showed him, through his dreams, *exactly* what he could expect if he continued to be a disappointment. Death was the least of these things. It whispered to him of what he was to do.

Pain seared through the young man's soul, eating him alive. He woke then, stifling a howl of fear and despair. The cold, serpent-smooth voice had given him a nearly impossible task. Seek out and slay the Keeper of the Deep Forest, on Argoth, in the heart of the Forest People's empire. The voice had given him the knowledge of 'how' to slay the great guardian. It seemed so simple, yet he knew that was not the case and he shivered, trembling to think of even contemplating such an act as the destruction of a demi-deity.

In the darkness of night he whimpered again, hugging himself. He seemed destined to be a disappointment to everyone he came in contact with. A strangled sob and the young man drew himself together. He pulled all of his unhappiness and fear into a ball and shoved it away. By morning all that was left were a burning anger, a gnawing bitterness, and the determination to carry out *this* task without fail.

Skycity Sevfahl, 10000ft above the Aeryth Ocean, Year of the Golden Hart, 2013 CE

Kalla kyl'Solidor snorted, thumping her staff against the ground in agitation as she strode down the corridor, red-trimmed black robes fluttering around her. Deep in the dim, dank depths of Dante's Inferno, the mage had come to seek a magister.

Culled from felons sentenced to death, a magister was bound to their mage, serving as a fierce and deadly protection, and as an extra conduit of power. Until now, Kalla had refused to take one. She felt that a mage should be capable of taking care of themselves, but the Sin' of Cryshal Kanlon disagreed, insisting that she follow tradition, and so she found herself in the pits of hell, following an overweight warden and forcing herself to ignore the lewd, sneering remarks of the prisoners they passed.

Dante's Inferno was arranged in a series of stacked levels, with the death row prisoners located at the bottom of the facility. She had been drug back and forth on a circuitous path through several levels so far and she was beginning to become annoyed. Kalla was fairly certain that there was a more direct route to the lower level and that the warden was just toying with her.

Kalla kyl'Solidor was a short female, with bright green eyes and jet-black hair, Argosian by birth. Though petite, the mage was filled to bursting with the power of her calling and the temper of her House. Despite her relatively young age, Kalla was already a maester, worthy of the prefix kyl' to her House name, skilled in healing, alchemy, and seership.

Kalla followed the warden down another spiraling staircase, but balked when he started to go down yet another shadowy corridor smelling of stale air and unwashed bodies.

"Enough! I have more important things to be doing today than traveling 'round and 'round through the dismal depths of Tartarus!" she snarled. The warden turned back, an oily smile plastered on his face.

"It is not much further, Lady, not much further," he said.

"That is what you said three levels ago. How many does the Inferno have?" Kalla's voice was low and cold. The warden scowled at her.

"Twelve levels, Lady kyl'Solidor," he replied in a sullen voice.

"Twelve... *Basa!* No more fooling around. We will go to Carron's Run now!" Reaching out, the mage touched the warden's forehead with the tip of her finger. An instant's discernment and she had a mental image of the Run. Another instant and she had transported them there.

Kalla shivered involuntarily, leaning against her staff to hide her sudden weakness. Teleportation took a great deal out of any mage, so much so that most did not even consider it in the worst of times, but Kalla was lucky in that it was another gift she excelled in. She scowled, glancing around, while the warden recovered from the impromptu trip.

Carron's Run, the death ward of the Inferno, was even darker, danker and smellier than the rest of the prison. Kalla held back as the warden walked the Run, bellowing for the inmates to line up at the cell doors, telling them what was expected. A low murmur of excitement and shuffling ensued. The chance to be a magister was a rare and lucky break for a criminal, one they weren't likely to pass up.

The warden finished his spiel and beckoned for her to examine the inmates. As Kalla passed by she could see the man was still wild-eyed. Her little demonstration of power had put things into a new perspective, giving him a greater respect, if not for her, then for the title she bore.

Kalla walked slowly up the corridor, silently examining her potential guardians, occasionally stopping for a closer look. None held any particular attraction and she wondered, not for the first time, *why* the magi used criminals to serve the role of magister. Oh, she knew the theory, but surely there were better options out there...

Twice she walked the length of the corridor before a soft coughing pulled her attention to a half-hidden door at the far end. Ignoring the warden's protests, she pushed the door open, wincing at the smell of urine, old blood and infection that washed over her. Beyond lay a small room with four tiny, cramped cells, much smaller than those outside. Three stood empty, doors slightly ajar. The fourth, however, contained a shirtless man chained to the wall, feet barely reaching the ground. He looked to be Arkaddian, with his coffee-colored skin and reddish-brown hair. It was unusual for any of the Plains people to be found in a skycity and she wondered how he had ended up here.

Kalla gave the man a more critical assessment. One eye was completely swollen shut and, if his wheezy breathing was any indication, he also had one or more fractured ribs. Dried blood crusted festering wounds along his face, arms and chest. Just barely visible under the aftermath of his new wounds Kalla could see a series of older scars, deep gashes across his chest and the top of one shoulder.

The mage frowned. Whatever the man had done, surely it could not be worth torturing him over. Were the conditions of confinement in the Run and the threat of imminent execution not enough?

"What crime has this man committed that he is locked here, in this state?" Kalla demanded. The man stirred at her words, peering at her through his good eye. The warden shuffled up beside her, nose wrinkling at the stench.

"This one is of no consequence, Lady kyl'Solidor," said the warden. The prisoner coughed again, wincing in pain.

"That does not answer my question." Kalla narrowed her eyes.

"What does it matter, Lady kyl'Solidor? This one is slated for execution within the hour." The warden's tone was surly.

A hoarse voice pulled her attention back to the cell.

"I am a thief, milady."

Said thief's voice was soft and lilting, despite the hoarseness. Kalla had guessed correctly- his accent bespoke an Arkaddian heritage.

"A... thief? You were tortured for being a thief? You are to be executed for stealing mere possessions?" Kalla's voice was incredulous. "Truly... how many did you kill to warrant this?" she asked. The man shook his head, grimacing with the pain of it.

"I killed no one, milady. I merely had the misfortune of being in the wrong place at the wrong time." He fell silent, bowing his head back down.

Beside her, the warden snorted.

"He assassinated the Lord Governor of Sevfahl," the pudgy man spat.

Kalla turned to regard the captive Arkaddian again. Just looking at him, she didn't judge him one capable of cold-blooded killing. Kalla released a whisper of power and the cell door creaked opened.

Deciding to find the truth of the matter out for herself, Kalla reached out and touched the prisoner gently on the forehead. He flinched away, but not before she'd gained enough of an insight to realize that the thief was telling the truth. An Arkaddian *had* assassinated the Lord Governor, unfortunately on the same night that *this* Arkaddian had decided to liberate a priceless artifact from the Governor's Palace. A feeling of familiarity lingered from the brief mind-touch, momentarily puzzling her.

Kalla growled, low and deep, fury igniting in her eyes. A whip-crack of power and the shackles unlocked. She caught the prisoner in coils of air, gently lowering him to the ground. The warden gave her a sullen look.

"Lord Tysin will not be pleased, Lady."

"I do not care about Lord Tysin's pleasure. The man speaks the truth. There were two Arkaddian visitors to the Palace that night, unlikely as that might seem. You caught a thief intent on nothing more than theft. Certainly not an offense worthy of such treatment. Your assassin is still free."

Kalla knelt down by the prisoner, where he now lay slumped against the wall. She ran gentle hands over him, assessing the damage. He had many wounds, but most were minor, certainly nothing she couldn't handle easily. Kalla studied him for a moment, then took a deep breath, fully committing herself to her course. Hand under his chin, Kalla raised his face to look at her.

"What is your name?" she asked softly.

"Ale... Aleister. Aleister Balflear." He attempted a wry grin. "The Sky Fox, at your service, milady."

"Well then, Aleister Balflear, I am Kalla kyl'Solidor and I am in need of a magister. What say you?"

A single brown eye widened, then he broke out in a fit of laughter that dissolved into another bout of coughing.

"Me? A magister? Milady, no offense, but I'm a thief, not a warrior. I fear you would be getting the short end of that deal," he replied.

"To be honest, I have no wish to take a magister at all, but the Powers that Be say I must. I'm not looking for brute strength. I value cunning and intelligence more and a fox should have more than enough of that." Her questioning look was rewarded with another half-smile.

"Very well, milady. If it keeps me from Tysin's clutches, I accept."

"You must be sure of this. Being magister to a mage means you are bound to them. I will be able to sense you, and you I. There will be times when I will need to rely upon you as a conduit of power, and times when I will need to rely on you for protection. If I should happen to die, so will you."

He nodded acceptance and sank back against the wall, his strength finally starting to fade.

"Then I guess I'd better make sure that doesn't happen anytime soon." There was the hint of a grin in his words.

"First things first. Let's get you healed." Kalla chased the warden out of the small room and closed the door. She took a few deep breaths, falling easily into the light trance needed for this relatively minor healing and rested her hands gently on the Sky Fox's chest.

Aleister tensed, then relaxed as soothing healing energy washed over him. Bones shifted, tiny fractures knitting together. The cuts healed, pushing the infection from them as they did so. The swelling receded, revealing a brown eye to match the other. Withdrawing her power, the healer surveyed her work. Aleister was much more presentable now, though blood and infection still clung to his skin. The cuts themselves were nothing more than shiny scars along his face, chest and arms.

Settling deeper into the trance, she focused on the man before her. Reaching out, Kalla placed both hands gently on Aleister's temples and carefully probed his mind. He tensed again, cringing away from the intrusion.

"Relax. Don't fight it. That will only cause pain," she whispered. Kalla felt him relax slowly, bit by bit. She didn't try to force her way into his mind, but waited until she felt he was more comfortable before forging the link.

The forging of the bond between mage and magister was a far cry from the brief mental touch she'd used on him earlier. In a sudden burst of power she tied the Sky Fox to her own essence. A feeling of déjà vu washed over her and she shook her head to clear it. As impossible as it was, the Sky Fox's very essence felt familiar to her. Fear and uncertainty flooded her mind and it took a moment before Kalla realized that what she felt belonged to Aleister rather than herself. Tightening her own mental shields, Kalla sent calmness to him. She felt Aleister pull his emotions under control, then a sense of gratitude from him for the stabilizing force.

Kalla drew back into herself, coming out of the trance to find a pair of warm brown eyes staring back at her. Aleister offered a shaky grin.

"Well, milady, I hope you don't come to regret your choice," he murmured with a wry look. Kalla sighed and shook her head, rising smoothly to her feet. She offered a hand and pulled the thief up. No, not a thief. A magister. *Her* magister.

"I see no reason why I should. You're a far more savory choice than some I've come across and I've been searching for quite some time to find a choice I was happy with. Come, let's get out of here and go get you cleaned up."

* * *

A mere twenty minutes later found Kalla back at the top of the Inferno. Sure enough, there was a much quicker way through the labyrinth than the warden had taken her before in the form of a small service elevator. Another of the Inferno's wardens had taken Aleister from her before they left the Run, escorting him through a different area. As he'd left, she'd felt his trepidation and a bit later his contentment. Shortly after she arrived at the entrance he reappeared, scrubbed clean and carrying what she assumed were the belongings he'd been brought in with.

Aleister was now dressed in simple, but well-made clothes. A slate-grey tunic fell to just above his knees, belted by a thin black belt from which hung three pouches and a long dagger. Comfortable black breeches brushed the tops of a pair of the soft-soled shoes so favored by the Arkaddians (and thieves most likely, Kalla mused). The shoes allowed the Plains warriors to walk soundlessly under any conditions.

The tunic had a low cut neck and peeking through she could see a *jinshin,* made of longtooth claws, with one of the long saber teeth of the great Plains cats as a centerpiece. Well, that would certainly explain the scars on his chest. Only Arkaddians who had undergone their Rite of Passage wore the *jinshin* as a mark of surviving. Young males were sent out into the Plains to face the longteeth and slay one, the bigger the better. If they survived, they were men. If not, they became food for the prides. Apparently her newly made magister had still been in Arkaddia when his time came.

"Well, now, don't you look much better." This earned her a dry chuckle.

"I certainly *feel* better, that's for sure." Aleister paused, looking towards the entrance gates. Kalla sensed puzzlement and a bit of loss.

"Milady, if I get my belongings back, does that include the *Stymphalian?*"

"*Stymphalian?*" she asked.

9

"My airship. She's not much- a converted Argosian strike-fighter."

Kalla nodded, taking note of his escort's grimace.

"All of your belongings should be returned, airship included. Guess they forgot to mention that."

Kalla turned to the new warden, favoring him with a flat look. He tugged at his collar nervously.

"The airship was confiscated. It was to be turned over to the new Lord Governor after the execution."

"Yes, well. Plans change and life goes on. There will be no execution and the Sky Fox is now a magister. He is entitled to have his ship back and if there is any damage to it I will be most unhappy. You will escort us to the paddocks if you please." Kalla's cold look brooked no argument.

They followed the unhappy warden down a long corridor and out into the open area of the airship paddocks. The ships of the Inferno lined the broad plaza. Most were small personal ships, though there were several bigger transports. Through the newly forged bond, Kalla felt Aleister's concern for his ship and she could sympathize. For those who made the sky their home, their ships were family. What she didn't understand was why one of the Plains people would have an airship in the first place. Aleister sighed in relief as he spotted the ship and took off at a trot towards it.

Kalla followed behind at a more sedate pace, emerald eyes sweeping the ship. The *Stymphalian* was a *Kruetzet*-class strike-fighter, equipped with twin ion cannon. She smiled wistfully. When she was younger, Kalla had learned to fly on the original *Kruetzet,* thanks to her military father. Her smile faltered. It had been years since she had thought of her father. When children blessed with magick were taken to the Kanlon, they lost all family ties. She had heard later, in her second year at the Kanlon, that her father had disappeared while on a mission. Neither ship nor captain had ever been found.

Kalla didn't know how her little thief-magister had managed to procure one of the ships, nor was she sure she really wanted to. Her people guarded their technology jealously and the Argosian Technomancers' magick was quite different from that of the Kanlon's Artificers.

Aleister was grumbling to himself as she approached, irritated that they had undone all of his careful security precautions. He fiddled with the hatch panel a bit more and the door hissed open, a thin set of stairs unfolding to allow entry. The Fox gave her a mischievous grin and started up the stairs.

"HEY! What do you think you're doing. That's *mine!*" A curly-haired teen was running towards them across the paddock-grounds. Kalla snorted. From the teen's angry voice and the commotion now commencing at the paddock entrance, she could only assume that Lord Tysin had arrived for the execution only to discover that the fox had slipped his trap. Indeed, even as the youth stopped before the *Stymphalian,* the crowd by the doors started towards them. The boy began to open his mouth again, but Kalla silenced him with a glare.

"The airship belongs to me now. I'm afraid that's something you are going to have to deal with, young man, unless you care to challenge the

Sin' of Cryshal."

"But it's MINE! Even the magi can't just take stuff!"

"Indeed. However, a magister's belongings go with him. The *Stymphalian* belongs to Aleister Balflear and Aleister belongs to me now, therefore the airship belongs to me," Kalla said in a flat voice. Before the boy could argue further, his father arrived, huffing and puffing.

"This is an OUTRAGE! I demand that you turn this *assassin* back over to me for execution. He killed our Lord Governor." Lord Tysin raged. Kalla's eyes narrowed.

"I'm sure the warden here has already explained things. You captured and tortured the wrong Arkaddian. This one is nothing more than a thief. Your assassin is still free.

Magi have the right to claim any criminal on a death-ward as their magister if they are in need. I was in need. Balflear is now my magister. No amount of outrage is going to change that." Kalla's voice was low, dangerous.

An unearthly wail interrupted her scolding, the sound rising and falling in the air. The paddocks abruptly erupted in flames as fireballs burst along the grounds, striking several of the airships. Lord Tysin and his son stumbled and turned to flee to the ironic safety of the Inferno, but a fireball engulfed them before they had taken two steps. Kalla beat a hasty retreat into the depths of the airship, where Aleister was already busy with the controls. The ship hummed to life as the engines engaged. Behind her, the door slid shut with a whisper of sound. Another fireball slammed into the pavement, rocking the ship. Kalla settled into the gunner's chair and buckled herself in.

"What the hell is going on?" the Sky Fox asked, his anxiety spilling over to her before he got it under control. There was a deep thrum within the ship as it lifted off from the paddock.

"I'm not sure." Kalla scanned the sky, finding nothing. Aleister pushed a few more controls and the ship's shield snapped into place just as a fireball washed over them. The *Stymphalian* rocked with the impact and he had to fight to keep control. Both of them screamed as the smoke cleared and brought them face to face with the source of the destruction. A brief glimpse of a nightmare visage of fangs and glittering orange scales and they had flown by the giant creature as its chest filled for yet another fiery assault.

"Fire wyvern," Kalla breathed, voice barely a whisper. It had been years since she had seen one. The fire wyvern were slender, serpentine creatures scaled in a fiery orange. Their tapered muzzles were graced with sensitive barbels and a sharp spike tipped the tail. Stubby horns framed the head, terminating in small spikes along the jaw line. Unlike dragons, wyvern lacked forelimbs, having only hindlimbs and an expansive set of wings.

Now that they were airborne, Kalla could see that the sky was filled with them. Odd, since they normally shunned human cities. The wyvern turned back to them and belched more fire at the ship, which Aleister deftly avoided. The creature bellowed in rage and dove after them, but the Sky Fox was living up to his name. He was quite the cunning pilot, but it was all he could do to avoid the beast's attacks. Kalla pulled the gunner's scope down and activated the strike-fighter's cannon.

"What are you doing!" Aleister yelped.

"Don't worry. Just fly!" Kalla tracked her target, then fired the cannon, one after the other. Both ion blasts slammed into the scaly creature, knocking it from the sky. Aleister whistled, impressed with her marksmanship. Kalla was equally impressed. The Arkaddian flew the ship better than some Argosians could, as if he had been born for it. Trusting Aleister to keep the ship safe, Kalla turned all of her attention and focus inward. She took two more of the wyvern down in quick succession, wincing as she did so. Like most Healers, she detested killing, even when it was necessary. Unfortunately the berserk creatures before her had no such compunctions. Two of them quickly paired up to tackle the airship together, forcing Aleister to become even more creative. Another fireball rocked the ship and a shrill warning alarm filled the cabin, followed by muffled curses from the magister.

"Another hit like that and the shields will be gone for good," Aleister's voice came out in clipped tones.

"Not if I can help it." Kalla divided her concentration, tracing the intricacies of the circuitry in her mind's eye, using her touch on the

controls as a guide. Finding the places that needed mending, Kalla drew just enough energy to repair the damage, never missing a beat with the cannon. By this time, the artillery of the Inferno's towers were at work, the giant anti-airship guns felling wyvern after wyvern. In short order, the battle was over. As Kalla came back to herself, Aleister turned the ship back to the paddocks. He let out a shaky sigh of relief and looked over at her.

"Where'd you learn to shoot one of these?" he asked.

"My father was captain of the original *Kruetzet*. I lived and breathed these ships growing up. Where'd you learn to *fly* one, Arkaddian?" she returned.

"I ran away from the Plainslands when I was young. Took up with an elderly Argosian who had turned to the life of a thief. He left me this ship."

There was a sadness to his thoughts and Kalla didn't press him for more information. Instead, she turned her attention to the destruction below. The Inferno's paddocks were littered with bodies, both human and wyvern alike, and crews ran over the grounds, trying to get the fires under control. Aleister banked the ship and circled again, seeking a safe place to land. He found one along the outer rim and brought the ship to ground.

They wasted no time in joining the crews seeking survivors, though these were few and far between. The air was filled with acrid smoke and the sickly sweet smell of burnt flesh. Most of those who had not perished from the flames were too badly damaged even for the mage to heal. The most she could do was make the passing easier. Dante's Inferno has certainly lived up to its name this day.

For hours she and Aleister worked among the dead and dying, until finally the sun began to set. Enormous Artifice lamps came on all across the paddocks, allowing the people to keep working. Kalla sighed as she turned away from yet another whose passing she had aided and leaned against Aleister for support. They paused to watch as chains were wrapped around the body of a wyvern. While others had been tending the wounded and the dead, prisoners had been brought out from the upper levels of the Inferno to aid in disposing of the giant bodies. Chains were wrapped around the corpses, hooked to the undercarriage of transport vessels and carried off.

A deep, rumbling growl sent the team around the body scurrying away amidst shouts that one of the beasts was still alive. Wardens came flocking to the area, bringing heavy rifles to bear on the weakly struggling creature. Kalla frowned as something caught her eye. A flash of silver glinted from beneath one of the wyvern's thick neckplates.

"Hold off."

Kalla gestured for the wardens to stay back and warily approached the wyvern. She talked softly and steadily, maintaining eye contact with the fiery-scaled creature. It snorted and tried to toss its head, but the chains weighted it down. She called the prisoners back.

"Grab the chains. Keep the head down." Kalla came closer, the fierce hawk-like eye following her every move. Behind her she could feel Aleister fairly dancing with anxiety as she carefully prised back one of the heavy neck scales. The wyvern bucked, throwing her back, but the prisoners quickly pulled the chains taut and she approached it again, still talking softly. Once more she prised the scale back, revealing a silvery knob lodged underneath. Kalla touched the object gently with her mind. It was embedded deep in the skin, like a giant metallic splinter. The area around the metallic splinter was inflamed and taught with infection. She beckoned Aleister over and had him take hold of the splinter.

"This... thing is tapped into the creature's spine. I want you to pull it out."

"Wouldn't it be better to wait until it's dead?" Aleister asked.

"I don't want it dead. I want to heal it. As you draw the pin out, I'm going to heal the wound behind it."

The Sky Fox gave her a look that said he thought she was crazy, but he waited until she'd settled into a healing trance, then gently started to pull the silver spike out. The wyvern twitched feebly, but did nothing more aggressive than growl at them. After what seemed like ages Aleister drew the point out. The entire thing was as long as his palm and, as he investigated it, he found that the tip was hollow and dripped the remains of an oily, green substance. Aleister carefully laid the spike to the side and turned back to Kalla. She was working now to heal the rest of the wyvern's injuries. Towards the end he started to feel a slight pull on his own energy reserves and from the fatigue he felt through the link between them, he guessed she was at her limit.

Kalla finished her work on the wyvern. She started to stand, and pitched forward suddenly, leaving her slumped against the giant creature's neck. It stirred and, with a movement swifter than a striking serpent, jerked its head free. The chains gave a metallic hiss as they slid to the ground and Kalla found herself wrapped in a haze of translucent red as the wing nearest curled around her. The great head dipped around to face her. Dimly Kalla heard Aleister yelling at the men to hold their fire, for fear that they would hit her instead. The wyvern snorted and smoky breath washed over Kalla.

You healed me. You saved me. Why?

Kalla could only gape in amazement at the distinctly feminine voice in her mind. Though credited with being extremely intelligent, it had never been noted that wyverns had anywhere near the sentience that their closest cousins- dragons- did.

"It's okay! Everything's okay! Don't shoot."

Kalla turned her attention back to the wyvern. "Your... people... are not known to be this aggressive to humans. When I saw the spike I assumed that it might have been part of the reason. I don't approve of killing simply for the sake of killing. It goes against all a magi Healer is taught. My name is Kalla kyl'Solidor."

The hawk eye blinked slowly.

I am Amaterasu, seer to the Cove Rock Clan and I thank you, both for healing me and for sparing my life. For that, my life belongs to you.

People came, many days ago, to the lands of the Cove Rock Clan. They came with guns that paralyzed us. They embedded the spikes in my people and we lost control of who we were.

Amaterasu shook her head, as if to clear it. *There was a voice in our minds. It whispered to us that we should leave our home. That we should attack the skycity. We were promised great riches and plentiful hunting, if we would do as we were bid.*

Grief filled the mage at the wyvern's words. She couldn't imagine who would do such a thing, to cause such death. If all of the wyvern's clan had attacked the Inferno, then Amaterasu was the last of her clan left alive.

"I don't know who would wish to cause such calamity. I've never seen anything like the spike, nor the drug used on you." Kalla laid her hand on the wyvern's neck. "If you trust us enough, I will do my best to get to the bottom of this and see those involved punished."

I thank you, Lady Mage. Amaterasu unfurled her wing, revealing Kalla to her relieved magister. There was a rustle of weapons as the wyvern levered herself upright, folding her wings about her body.

"There is no need to worry. This wyvern we have no need to fear. She will harm no one," Kalla said.

"*She?* How can you tell if it's a *she?* And how do you know it won't attack again?" One of the wardens was brave enough to question the mage.

"She told me, that's how." Kalla allowed Aleister to help her up, ignoring the puzzled looks all around her.

"You need to rest, milady. You've done enough for today. I'm sure quarters can be found for you in the Inferno," said Aleister. Kalla shook her head.

"No... if the *Stymphalian* still has her living quarters, it is there I would prefer to rest," she replied in a drowsy voice. All Argosian ships had living quarters in them. The *Kruetzet* had featured two tiny sleeping rooms, one for the captain and one for the gunner. In addition, there had been a tiny bathroom area complete with a cramped shower, a tiny 'kitchen' and a cargo area. Aleister nodded and guided her back up the ship's stairs, to one of the small berths. He took the staff from her and made to help her onto the bed, but she waved him away.

"This isn't right...," Kalla mumbled. She reached out and touched the bunk, pulling a small amount of strength from Aleister as she did so. The air shimmered and the bed disappeared, reforming into a hammock like the ones that had originally been on the ship. Kalla swayed on her feet, hardly aware of Aleister scooping her up and putting her in the hammock. Hardly aware of his good-natured grumbling as he did so.

"...I can see why they wanted you to have a magister... I have my work cut out for me. Do you always overdo things?" muttered Aleister as he gently covered her with a blanket and crept from the small quarters.

* * *

Morning found the paddocks cleared of bodies, if not of debris. Kalla yawned and stretched as she stood in the ship's doorway. She had to admit, sleeping in the safety and security of the *Kruetzet*-class ship had been wonderfully relaxing, though she had been a bit put out that the hammocks had been removed. It had been a foolish risk to completely drain herself to change it back, but she'd slept better for it and was now completely recovered.

A thud behind the ship brought her out of her musings, and a fiery-scaled head dipped around the side. A fierce orange eye fixed itself on her.

Good morning, Lady Mage.

"Good morning, Amaterasu. Don't be so formal. It's just Kalla," the Healer said.

As you wish, Lady... Kalla. I am bid give you a message. The grumpy male went to get food. He said that they had taken the metal bird's stores. He will be back soon.

He slept not last night, Lady Mage. He was worried that you had overdone yourself.

Kalla frowned and cast her mind in search of her magister. She found him in the Inferno and he was indeed grumpy and tired. Worry tinged his thoughts and she felt a momentary twinge of guilt. The young mage was not used to having another concerned for her well-being. Before, it had just been her, looking out for herself. She often did push herself past her limits, but before she'd had the safety of the Kanlon in which to regain her strength and unlike most magi, she could recover her power in a few hours, rather than the many hours to days that it took other magi so completely drained of energy.

Kalla had another level of protection, too. She had gained the nickname 'Wolf that Sleeps' long ago, because she was prone to strike out at people who disturbed her in her sleep- the calculating and deadly attack of a disturbed frost wolf. Strength had bred in her a certain flippancy and casual attitude towards her own welfare. Kalla supposed that was one reason the Sin' had insisted she take a magister.

Irritation filtered through the link as Aleister dealt with the Inferno officials. No doubt they still harbored resentment over the fact that he had been freed from 'justice'. Kalla shook her head and turned her attention back to the wyvern looming over the ship.

"Amaterasu, you said last night that you were the seer of the Cove Rock Clan. I would like to do a scrying, to try and find some answers or at least a starting point. I would appreciate your help. Two minds are always better than one," she said. The wyvern nodded.

If you can scry by fire, Lady Mage, then I can help. I'm sorry to say, I know no other way.

"Fire is fine. And it's just Kalla." the mage replied absently, turning her gaze to the doors as she sensed Aleister heading back their way. He trudged across the paddock grounds, his arms laden with bags and packages. Kalla went to meet him and collected some of the packages.

"I see you're awake, milady. Did you recover your strength?" he asked.

"Aye, I did. It never takes long. And it's just Kalla! Why do all of you insist on calling me anything *but* that," she grumbled. Kalla followed her magister up the steps, turning back to the wyvern before going into the ship. "Give me a bit, Amaterasu, and we can begin. Breakfast wouldn't hurt first."

"Begin what...?" The Sky Fox's voice was weary. He took the supplies from her and began stashing them in the necessary compartments.

"Amaterasu and I are going to do a fire scrying, to seek out the cause of this." She caught his frown. "Don't worry. I'll be fine. I'm fully recovered. You, however, should get some sleep." Kalla paused for a moment and her voice was soft when next she spoke. "Thank you for keeping watch. I will try my best to not overdo things in the future. I've gotten so used to it just being me."

Aleister had gone still while she'd been speaking. Kalla felt a bit of fear through the bond, but mostly she felt a sadness. He quelled it quickly, burying it behind his mental shields. Kalla had to admit- he was getting better at keeping his emotions from spilling over too much.

"Bloody wyvern," he muttered under his breath, turning back to the kitchen area.

"Yes, Amaterasu did tell me you'd been up all night, but I would have figured it out anyway. Your mind is grumpy when you're tired," she laughed. The Sky Fox gave her an indignant look.

"I am *not* grumpy," he huffed. She laughed again, the sound ringing through the ship.

"I rest my case. Go relax a bit. I can fix our breakfast. I do know my way around these ships, remember?" she chided gently. Aleister turned over the kitchen to her, grumbling as he made his way to the front, where he flopped down in the captain's chair. Within minutes he was dozing peacefully and Kalla didn't have the heart to wake him when she was finished making breakfast. Instead she conjured a covered tray, charmed it to keep the food hot, and left it on the counter.

Kalla found Amaterasu at the far end of the paddock, where the wyvern had already collected a pile of debris together. When she saw Kalla approaching she swelled up and spat flame at the pile, igniting a roaring bonfire.

I trust this will be satisfactory, Lady Mage.

"It's perfect. Will you allow me to link my mind to yours? That will make things go more smoothly," Kalla said. When the wyvern nodded assent, Kalla reached out and put a hand on the muzzle before her, sending a bit of her own essence to join with Amaterasu's in a simple scrying link. Thus bonded, the two settled before the fire, letting the hypnotic flames lull them into a trance. Scenes began to form in the dancing flames - people with tranquilizer rifles, sneaking into the lands of the wyvern, impaling them with the spikes. They melted away and were replaced by scenes of the same wyvern clans attacking skycities all around the world of De Sikkari. One city, though it managed to take out all of its assailants, still fell to the flames of destruction.

Kalla recognized it. The skycity of Ben'talen had been completely destroyed.

They saw Argoth's response, the great flagships with smaller strike-fighters swarming around them. Few of the skycity's attackers managed to get near enough to do damage to the land itself. Kalla recognized the flagships *Kujata, Fenrir, Barghast* and *Tengu,* as well as the Grand Flagship *Phoenix.*

Skycity after skycity they saw, most faring as Sevfahl had. There were other scenes in which humans spiked land-bound creatures and set them to attacking ground cities. Some fell, some survived. More of those attackers survived, running off into the wilds to nurse their wounds.

The scene shifted again, coalescing into images of a statue of monolithic proportions, whose eyes glowed with a radiant malevolence. Coil upon mythril coil glittered in the dark light. Another shift and they saw the same great creature, a Nagali, alive and in the flesh. A winged warrior drove home a spear whose tip was bound in parchment, impaling the beast in the heart, turning it to mythril. Images of a white feather, a palace in the mountains, a spear with a two-foot point. Kalla knew without knowing, what they needed to find to use against the creature, that they would need to face the fearsome Nagali. The vision began to fragment, but the final image that came to the linked minds was of a terrible cataclysm and a land sunk beneath the waves.

Slowly the two came back to themselves. Kalla broke the link and leaned against Amaterasu's side.

"Mercy of Balgeras... if I understand right, the Nagali is waking. It was he who sent the humans to the wyvern and the wyvern to their deaths in the sky," she breathed. Amaterasu growled, a long, low sound.

Al'dhumarna. Bound aeons ago on the Isle of Whispers. If he truly be waking, then we are in terrible danger. It is the Nagali's delight to cause havoc and destruction. We must recreate the binding of old, in order to stop him.

"But how... in the legends the Nagali was bound by a scroll penned by the Elephant Lord, using the Quill of Ma'at. The white feather. And by using the weapon called Grael's Fang, said to be forged from a tooth of the Dragon Goddess herself. I have no idea where to even begin looking for such mythic artifacts."

Kalla paused, thoughtful. "We should consult Gasta, the Keeper of the Deep Forest on Argoth. If any can point us in the right direction, it will be the Keeper."

Skycity Sevfahl, 10000ft above the Aeryth Ocean, Year of the Golden Hart, 2013 CE

Kasai watched from his perch atop the highest ramparts of the Inferno as his scapegoat walked back across the paddocks to the Argosian ship. He chuckled to himself. Now that had been a lucky break, finding another trespasser to take the fall for him after he'd carried out the assassination. Lucky break for the other, too, that the mage had come just in time to save him.

The Arkaddian uncoiled his wiry frame, running a hand over a scarred face. Kasai favored the looks of his people, save for the fact that his right eye was the color of mahogany, glinting with red highlights in the light. The left eye had been taken long ago, in battle. All that was left was a milky orb that saw nothing. The scars were a source of pride, the mark of a true warrior. His shoulder length red-brown hair was pulled up in a traditional Arkaddian bob.

Kasai was one of the Khan's Harriers, an elite group that served as guards, assassins, information gatherers. The Harrier adjusted the slender swords across his back and slipped away into the shadows, lips curling at the mere thought of the assassination he'd been forced to carry out. He'd bet good vykr that the order hadn't really come from the Khan himself, but had been instigated by the mage that came to Karokorum quite often of late. Kasai wondered who the other Arkaddian was and how he'd come to be on Sevfahl in the first place.

Dashmar, Evalyce, Year of the Golden Hart, 2013 CE

Merryn crept quietly down the smooth stone corridor and edged into a small work chamber off the left. It was the middle of the night and the room was lit only by a pair of gently flickering glowlamps. A small furnace stood in one corner, the door slightly open, radiating heat into the workroom. The lamps cast eerie dancing shadows along the walls and floor, making it seem as if the night air itself were alive.

A long, low table ran the length of one wall, tools arranged neatly over it. A handful of uncut gems- sapphires, rubies, emeralds, diamonds, even a single multi-hued zarconite- were piled upon a velvet pouch, glittering in the dim light like dragons' scales. Merryn froze as the man sitting hunched over the table sat back and stretched, running a hand through thick blond curls, before returning to his work.

Absorbed in his project, he gave no indication that he heard her enter and Merryn curled up quietly in the far corner. From her vantage point the area before him was visible and she could see that he was painstakingly shaping an emerald. The man was Merryn's husband, but the marriage had been purely political. She gave a barely audible sigh. She'd tried, she really had, to make things work, but he paid her little mind. Small wonder that he didn't notice her the occasions she did sneak into the workroom. She knew he would probably be angry if he found her, especially this time of the night, but she couldn't help herself. She wanted to be close to him. And she could hope things improved... Merryn watched him work and wove dreams of a happier future until she fell asleep, propped against the wall.

The blond-haired man slipped the jeweler's loupe from thin-rimmed glasses and let it fall to thump dully against his chest. He took it from around his neck and tucked it away into its proper place. The glasses quickly followed suite. Running his hands over his face, he yawned. Hours had slipped away during his crafting. Trapped in the depths of the caverns, he had little idea of the true time but he suspected it was early morning. Putting his tools away, he surveyed his final product- a leaf-shaped emerald set into a ring base. It winked green fire at him as he turned it this way and that, assessing the soundness of it.

Satisfied, he put the ring into a velvet pouch containing a similar one cut from carnelian and tucked the pouch into his robes. Rising stiffly, he turned to leave and heaved a sigh as he realized his young wife was sound asleep in the corner. Usually he heard her enter, even though he rarely acknowledged it, but tonight he'd been too lost in his work.

There were times when he wondered *why* he had agreed to the marriage to begin with. Among a people to whom such alliances mattered not at all, theirs was an unusual partnership indeed. A very surprising and unlikely one whose proposal had thrown him off guard. Merryn deserved more than a man with the chains he bore about his neck, but he'd needed to keep this particular alliance and so he found himself with a young woman nearly ten years his junior, whom he had no idea what to do with.

He didn't imagine that Merryn was very happy with her situation either, given that his attitude towards her tended to be brusque to the point of disdain, but she seemed drawn to him like a moth to flame so often did she creep into his workroom. It wasn't that he hated her. Far from it. It had simply been so long since he'd cared about anything that his heart had forgotten how. Stifling a twinge of regret, he carefully picked her up. Merryn made a small noise of protest at being moved and burrowed her head against him. With a deep breath, she lapsed once more into sleep. Carrying her back to their room, he tucked her beneath the blankets and collapsed into exhausted slumber beside her.

Seeking Gasta

Kalla yawned, shifting position in the gunner's seat. She glanced out the window, smiling at the sight of Amaterasu's graceful swooping around the ship. The wyvern had had no trouble keeping pace with the strike-fighter, even over long distances.

As they approached the outermost boundaries of Argoth's skyspace, they were greeted by the flagship *Kujata,* strike-fighters swarming around her like bees around a hive. Static crackled on the radio.

"*This is the Imperial Flagship* Kujata. *Identify yourselves.*"

Aleister gave her a wry look.

"So much for blending in," he said, reaching for the radio. "This is the *Stymphalian,* requesting permission to enter Argosian skyspace. We have business on the mainland. The wyvern is with us!" The last was added hastily when he noticed several of the fighters were making a beeline for Amaterasu. His message must have been relayed, as they broke off and went back to circling the flagship.

"*Argoth's boundaries are closed. No one is allowed through.*"
The voice sounded apologetic. Kalla gestured for the radio and
Aleister turned it over.

"This is Kalla kyl'Solidor, of House Solidor. I have urgent need
to reach Argoth. If needed, send an escort with us, but we must
reach the mainland." There was a long pause before the radio
came to life again, and when it did it was no less than the *Kujata's* Admiral himself.

"*Lady kyl'Solidor, this is Admiral Ventaal Karlgraffsson. We
must acquire permission of the* Phoenix *before we allow you to
pass. Please bring your ship into the* Kujata."

"Thank you, Admiral. We shall do so." Kalla put the radio back
as Aleister guided the ship into one of the *Kujata's* numerous
docking bays, passing easily through the airshield that kept the
workers safe when the bay doors were open. Strike fighters of
many different classes filled the bay in neat, orderly rows. The
bay flagmen guided them to an empty spot and Aleister snugged
the *Stymphalian* into place as neatly as one of the military pilots
might have. The flagmen gave nods of approval.

Amaterasu had followed them inside, but hung back by the
hanger doors. The Argosians in the hanger gave her a wide
berth, nervous as horses near fire to be in the presence of the
great creature.

An aide scurried up to Kalla and Aleister, bowing to them.

"Greetings Lady kyl'Solidor. Admiral Karlgraffsson will see
you in the great-room," he murmured. Kalla gave Amaterasu
a wave, which the wyvern returned with a solemn nod, and
turned to follow the aide. The great-room lived up to its name. It
was a large room containing an immense table of burnished oak
surrounded by plush chairs. The Admiral was at the far end of
the room. He looked up as they entered and dismissed the aide,
who snapped a salute and left.

"Well, well. If it isn't little Kally returned home." Ventaal had
dropped all pretense of formality once the aide had left. Hazel

eyes twinkled in delight and he wrapped her in a bear hug when they reached him. Kalla chuckled to herself as she felt Aleister's alarm.

"What brings you back to Argoth, Kalla? Official business for the Kanlon?" Ventaal turned to regard Aleister. "And who is this fine, young gentleman?"

"Something like that, Ventaal. This is Aleister, my magister," she replied. Ventaal gave the Sky Fox a hearty handshake and an appraising look.

"Magister, huh. So they finally made you get one?" the Admiral asked in a jovial voice. Ventaal turned back to Aleister. "I don't envy you, son. You're going to have your hands full."

Kalla could fairly hear Aleister's teeth grinding.

"Yessir, I've already figured that out," he muttered. Ventaal laughed and Kalla turned a scathing look on the pair of them.

"If you two are quite done now... perhaps we might discuss business?" Kalla growled, earning more muted laughter.

"How long do you think it will take to get permission for us to travel to Argoth, Ventaal. We need to go to the Deep Forest," Kalla asked.

The Admiral shuddered. "Why on earth would you want to go there, Kalla?"

"Argoth was not the only skycity assaulted, Admiral. We seek answers as to the 'why' and I believe I may find some with the Keeper of the Forest."

"It shouldn't take too long, not with the request coming from a mage, though we will likely have to escort you in, especially with the company you keep. Why do you have one of those beasts with you?"

Kalla sank into one of the plush chairs and told her friend of the events at Sevfahl and her healing of Amaterasu. While the Admiral was pondering over what they had told him, the intercom came to life.

"Admiral? The Phoenix *has granted our request. We are to send a quarti-talon of fighters with them in escort."*

"Very well. Advise the pilots to make ready." Ventaal turned to Kalla. "I assume you'll want to leave right away?"

"Yes, Admiral, that would be nice. The sooner, the better. I want answers."

"Just so. I hope you find them." Vetaal wrapped her in another hug. "Take care, Kally."

The Admiral turned to shake Aleister's hand again. "It's been a pleasure to meet you, Aleister." His look turned serious. "Take good care of her, magister."

The Admiral himself led them back to the hanger. He gave their ship a once-over as they crossed the bay to the *Stymphalian.*

"*Kruetzet*-class. Good ships. I'm not even going to ask how you managed to get your hands on one." Ventaal slapped the side of the ship affectionately. He started to walk away, then turned back, an odd look on his face. "I could swear I've seen this ship before." He waved the thought away and bid the pair farewell. "Good journey and good luck, Lady Kalla!"

Kalla returned a wave and a nostalgic smile, before climbing the *Stymphalian*'s stairs. Ventaal had been one of her father's dearest friends. He had been as close as family before Kalla had gone to the Kanlon and seeing the Admiral again brought back painful memories and the guilt that she had never gotten to say 'good-bye'. The mage sank down into the gunner's chair without a word, lost in thought.

Aleister powered the ship back up and smoothly lined up to follow their escort out the doors, casting a worried glance at his broody companion. Kalla kept to her thoughts as they traveled the final distance to Argoth. Aleister's soft, lilting voice drug her from her reverie as they approached the skycity.

"We are here, milady."

The mage looked up to see the skycity loomed ahead of them. Though called 'skycity', Argoth was in fact a sky continent, an Empire ruled by House Sykes. It was strange to be back home. Kalla had not set foot on Argoth since she had left to become a mage. She had not even returned after she had become a full maester and was free to leave the Kanlon on her own. Her father had been missing and declared dead many years by that time and returning was too painful for her. It still was, but now it was necessary.

Kalla became more watchful as the great guns of the Outer Wall tracked them, ready to take them down if they proved hostile. The Trinity Claw banners of House Sykes snapped and fluttered all along the length of the great Wall. In the distance she could just make out another of the great flagships, with its attendant swarm of fighters. By the shape, it looked to be the *Fenrir.*

Aleister followed the escort into one of the military paddocks lining the Outer Wall, bringing the *Stymphalian* into line with the others. Amaterasu landed, coiling protectively around the ship. A large, official procession was already at the paddocks, waiting to receive them. The lead dignitary bowed to them and Kalla gave a half-bow back. Though Kanlon magi were above royalty, it never hurt to pay respects.

"Greetings, Lady kyl'Solidor. Greetings Magister Balflear. The Admiral has informed us of your mission. Passes, supplies and mounts have been obtained for you." He glanced up at Amaterasu. "I am sorry, Lady Amaterasu, but I must ask that you stay here. Given recent events, it would not be a good idea for you to be away from the protection of the Imperial forces."

The wyvern nodded, bringing her head down to his level. He flinched back.

Tell him, if they can feed me and allow me to stretch my wings, then I do not mind waiting with the ship.

Kalla relayed the message and the dignitary visibly relaxed. Clearly, he had expected this to be a sticking point. If Kalla had insisted, they would have had to let the wyvern accompany them, but she could see the wisdom in avoiding unnecessary conflict. Besides, the vykr mounts would not be controllable in the presence of such a predator.

"We will be back as soon as we can, Amaterasu. Please keep the *Stymphalian* safe for us."

The wyvern let out a rumbling assent that caused the assembled escort to shrink back.

I will do so, Lady Mage. Be safe and come back soon.

"We'll try our best. It will take about a week and a half to reach the Deep Forest, but no telling how long until we find Gasta. The Keeper can be hard to find if he doesn't want company," Kalla replied.

I will try to be patient, Lady Mage. May the wind guide your wings. The wyvern's voice rumbled through her mind. Kalla put a hand to her muzzle.

"Thank you, Amaterasu. I pray it will be so," said Kalla.

Kalla and Aleister followed the escort across the paddock and through the checkpoints of the Outer Wall. They were given Imperial passes to aid them when they came to towns, packs full of the necessary supplies, and a pair of vykr.

The beasts snorted uneasily, stamping their hooves. Vykr were sturdy creatures, with a stocky build. They had a single, stubby spiral horn in the center of their foreheads and were covered in a thick, shaggy pelt of black fur. Aleister grinned, patting the vykr on their velvety noses. He spoke softly to them and they calmed. The Arkaddian handled the beasts as if they were old friends. Vast herds of vykr were kept by the nomadic Arkaddian Empire and he had no doubt learned to work with the hardy creatures at a very young age.

Kalla took his hand, pressing hers over it. It was a matter of mere concentration to create a few small cubes of sugar in his palm. She stepped back, twitching a small smile as the vykr pressed against him, eager for the sweet treat. Kalla and her magister swung themselves up into the saddles, bid farewell to the Imperial escort, and made their way through the gates.

Argoth, 10000 ft. above the Aeryth Ocean, Year of the Golden Hart, 2013 CE

Kalla sighed and slid from the saddle, stretching as she did so and slipping her staff from its tether. Nearby, Aleister climbed down, mirroring his mage's stretch. They had stopped before the Dancing Bear Inn, one of the finer ones in the small town of Millan. A stable boy came to take the vykr away. His eyes widened when he realized she was a mage and he tugged a forelock in respect.

"Take your vykr, Lady Mage?" the stableboy asked. Kalla smiled and handed him the reins. Aleister did likewise.

"Dos mere…" Her voice trailed off questioningly.

"My name is Pip, Lady Mage," the boy said. Kalla made a gesture, plucking a small coin from thin air.

"Well, then, Pip. Take good care of our vykr and there will be one of these for you now and one when we leave."

The boy's eyes grew wider as she handed the coin over to him. It was likely more than his wages for a month. She winked conspiratorially. "It'll be our secret. The innkeep need never know."

His eyes lit up. "I'll take the bestest care of them, Lady Mage!" Pip led the animals to the stable, back straight with pride. Kalla chuckled softly as she and Aleister went into the inn, packs slung over their shoulders.

Conversation died away as everyone craned to get a look at the newcomers. The innkeep hurried forward, wiping his hands on his apron. He was a chubby man with a good-natured face and his establishment seemed every bit as welcoming as he was, for the gazes weren't hostile, merely curious.

"How may I help you, Lady Mage?" He dipped a bow.

"We'd like rooms for the night, Master Innkeep. Dinner would be nice too, if it's not too much trouble."

"No trouble at all, Lady Mage, no trouble at all. My name is Wylsin. Will you eat here or dine in your rooms?"

Kalla glanced around the inn's common room. It was pleasantly crowded.

"My name is Kalla kyl'Solidor and this is my magister, Aleister Balflear. We'll eat down here, if you please."

Master Wylsin gestured for one of his assistants to take their packs and led them to a table in the corner.

"Something to drink then, Lady Mage? Magister?"

"Fury wine, if you have any," said Kalla. Aleister gave her an incredulous look.

"Oh, gods be good. Well, I'm not going to try to compete with that... I'll have fire whiskey, Master Wylsin."

The innkeep chuckled.

"Indeed we do, Lady Mage. Your drinks and dinner will be right out." Wylsin bustled off into the kitchen, cheerfully yelling to the staff. Aleister turned back to her, one eyebrow raised slightly.

"Fury wine, milady? Are you sure that's such a good idea?" he asked. Despite its name, fury wine was not a wine at all, but one of the most potent alcoholic beverages in all of De Sikkari. The best came from the distilleries on Port Jericho.

"Magi aren't affected quite the same way by alcohol. It takes a great deal more to cause even a pleasant buzz. Hence the fury wine. It is a built in protection for magi. It comes with the magick. Think the damage a mage not in full control of their powers might wreak. Don't worry- that immunity will pass on to you as well, now you're a magister."

Aleister shook his head, muttering to himself, something fast becoming a trend. Wylsin arrived with a fine dinner of roast mutton, soft brown bread covered in butter, Argosian wild rice and a twelve bean salad. The pair ate quietly, content to watch the crowd. Aleister finished first. He pushed his plate away and relaxed, resting his chin against his hand. The fire whiskey had left him relaxed and content, the feelings filtering over to Kalla. Another emotion ran undercurrent, though she couldn't tell just what. He was unconsciously dampening it, but the fire whiskey had weakened his control enough that she felt it intermittently.

Kalla chuffed a laugh as she noticed what he was watching. At a nearby table a game of *kessala* was in progress. The dice game was popular among the Argosian military and Aleister had no doubt learned it from his previous companion. She gestured to the table.

"Go join them. I'll let you know before I go upstairs," she said.

"Are you sure you don't mind?" the Fox asked. Kalla yawned, finally starting to feel the effects of the fury wine.

She nodded. "I'm sure. Go on."

Aleister gave her a mock salute and the feeling of familiarity overcame her again, as it had in the Inferno. As if the pair of them had played this same scenario out before.

"Thanks, captain," he said. Kalla snorted as she watched him thread through the tables, where he was readily accepted into the dicing circle. Extracting a slim journal and a pen from a hidden pouch inside her robes, Kalla spent the next few moments writing before a tug on her robes broke her concentration. She looked down to see a tiny girl standing by her knee. Two more children stood farther back, too shy to approach the mage.

"Yes, little one? Can I help you with something?" Kalla asked.

The little girl blushed and scooted her toe in the dirt.

"Can you tell us a story, Lady Mage? Mages have the best stories!"

Kalla couldn't help but smile. While bardcraft wasn't her particular interest she wasn't a half bad storyteller. Kalla nodded and gestured for the children to gather around her. They all shuffled forward and found places in the floor before her.

"I think I can spare a story. What kind of story do you want to hear?"

"Magick!" A chorus of little voices chanted back to her.

"Well now, I'm sure I can find something to fit the bill," Kalla said as she settled into her storyteller mode.

"Once, long ago, when the world was young and the creatures new-made, all things were wild, even the Tame Creatures. The Vykr was wild, the Goat was wild and the Booa was wild. So, too, were the Geese and the Mir'aj. But the wildest of the wild was the Sabretooth, the little cousin of the Longtooth. The Sabretooth, he walked by himself and no place was closed to him.

"Of course, Man was wild too. Terribly so. It took Woman to tame Man, for she would not live Man's wild ways. Woman it was who found a nice, dry cave, a cave within Berkhat Keldon, to dwell in, rather than lay her head wherever she be. She strew clean sand and made rush pallets for bedding. At the far end of the cave, she made a warm fire and before the opening to the cave she placed the skin of a Pronghorn, that the winds and rains might not enter the home of the Woman and the Man.

"That night they feasted upon wild sheep flavored with garlic and pepper, roasted upon the fire. With it they had shilan mushrooms, wild-rice and the fruits of the Plains. After the fine meal, Man was content and he went to sleep before the fire, but Woman, she was not content.

"She stayed up, thinking. As she thought, she whittled a flute from a bone of the pronghorn. And then? Then the Woman made magick, the first magick the world had ever known and a magick now lost. It was Woman that birthed the magick of the True Harpers, the magick of the Spellsingers. She played a song upon her bone flute, a song of her needs, her wishes, her desires and one by one they came to her.

"Out upon the vast plains the Wild Ones gathered together where they could see the fire from a long distance and they wondered what it meant for them. Wild Vykr stamped his foot upon the ground in agitation.

"*My friends and my enemies, why have Man and Woman made a great fire in the cave of Keldon and what does it mean for us?*" he asked.

Wild Booa lifted his nose to the winds and caught the scent of roasting pronghorn. Finding it pleasing, he decided to investigate.

"*I will go and I will look, for I do believe it a good thing. Sabretooth, come with me!*" Wild Booa exclaimed. Sabretooth merely sniffed.

"*Nay, I am Sabretooth who walks alone and all places are the same to me. I will not come.*" replied Sabretooth.

"*Then no more shall we be friends,*" replied Wild Booa and with that he trotted off to the cave. But Sabretooth was curious, as all his

kin are, and he found himself stealthily following Wild Booa. At the cave he hid himself and watched as Wild Booa approached and cautiously poked his nose beneath the door hanging. When Woman caught sight of him she thought to herself, 'well, here is the first.'

"*Welcome Wild One of the Wild Plains. What is it that you seek?*" Woman asked.

"*Wife of my enemy, what is that that smells so good?*" Wild Booa asked. At this, Woman picked up a haunch of the roast meat and threw it to the Wild Booa.

"*Wild One of the Wild Plains, taste and see for yourself,*" she said. Wild Booa gnawed the bone and it was more delicious than anything he had ever tasted. When he was done, he begged Woman for another.

"*Wild One of the Wild Plains, go with Man by day to hunt and guard our lands and guard this cave, our home, by night and I shall give you all the bones you desire,*" Woman replied. Wild Booa agreed, for he thought the deal a good one and from that day on he was no more Wild Booa, but simply Booa, he who would become the guardian of the herds.

"*Aah,*" thought Sabretooth. "*This is a wise Woman, but she is not so wise as I.*" And with a swish of his tufted tail, Sabretooth sauntered out into the Plains, thinking Booa to be very foolish for having given up his freedom.

"When the Man woke the next morning and spied Booa he said, "*What is Wild Booa doing here?*" To which Woman replied, "*His name is not Wild Booa, but rather, it is First Friend, because he will be our friend for always and always. Take him with you when you go hunting.*"

"The next day, Woman collected great armfuls of green grass from the grassy seas and lay them by the door, so that the air smelt of fresh cut grass. She sat weaving a halter from sturdy grass fronds and when she was done, she once more played her Song on the bone flute.

"Out on the Wild Plains, Wild Vykr stamped his hoof, agitated by the absence of Wild Booa and tempted by the smell of new cut grass drifting over the Plains. He decided to see what had become of Wild Booa. Once more Sabretooth followed in stealth and hid himself

nearby. Trotting up to the Cave, Wild Vykr stopped before Woman.

"*Greetings Wild One of the Wild Plains. What seek you here?*" she asked.

"*Wife of my enemy, where is Wild Booa? What have you done with him?*" Wild Vykr asked.

"*Wild One of the Wild Plains, you did not come here for the sake of Wild Booa, but for the green grass I have here.*"

"*This be true,*" Wild Vykr said, for indeed it was. "*Give it to me to eat.*"

"*Very well, Wild One, come to me. Bend down your wild head and wear that which I will put upon you and you shall eat the fresh cut grass thrice daily.*" Woman said. Wild Vykr came near, allowing the Woman to slip the halter around his neck. Bending his head down, Wild Vykr touched his horn to the ground in submission.

"*Oh my Mistress and wife of my Master, I will be your servant, for the sake of the wonderful grass,*" Wild Vykr said and from that day forward he was Wild Vykr no longer but simply Vykr, the mount and companion to those who would be rulers of the Plains.

"*Aah,*" thought Sabretooth. "*This is a clever Woman, but she is not so clever as I.*" And with a swish of his tufted tail, Sabretooth sauntered out into the Plains, thinking Vykr to be very foolish for having given up his freedom.

"When Man and Booa came back from hunting that evening and spied the Vykr, Man said, "*What is Wild Vykr doing here?*" To which Woman said, "*His name is not Wild Vykr any longer, but rather First Servant, because he will carry us from place to place for always and always. Ride on his back when you go hunting.*"

"The next day Wild Goat came to the Cave and as before, Sabretooth followed and hid himself to watch what would happen. Everything happened just as it had before and when Wild Goat promised to provide the Woman with warm milk in exchange for wonderful grass, Sabretooth said the same things as before. And just as before, Sabretooth sauntered out onto the Plains savoring his freedom.

"Next day, Sabretooth waited to see which of the Wild Ones would approach the cave, but none dared. Finally he decided to go himself and found Woman there milking Goat. When she saw him, she said,

"*Wild One of the Wild Plains, I have not summoned you. I have put up the magick flute as we have no more need for either friends or servants.*"

"At this Sabretooth lashed his tail. "*I am neither friend nor servant. I am Sabretooth, he who walks alone, and I wish to come into your cave.*"

"*If that be the case, why then did you not come with Booa, the first night?*" Woman asked. "*You are Sabretooth, he who walks by himself, and all places are alike to you. You are neither a friend nor a servant. You have said it yourself. Go away and walk by yourself in all places alike.*"

"At this Sabretooth pretended to be sorry and asked, "*Must I never be allowed into the cave? Never to sit by the warm fire as Booa does? Beautiful lady, you could not be cruel, even to a Sabretooth.*"

"*Beautiful lady am I? Very well then, I will make you a bargain. If ever I say one word in your praise, that is when you may come into the cave,*" Woman replied.

"*And if you should say two words?*" Sabretooth asked.

"*If I should say two words, then not only may you come into the cave, but you may stay and curl up by the fire as Booa does.*"

"*Very well. I shall remember,*" Sabretooth said and took himself off to the Plains. There he stayed for a very long time, until the Woman had long since forgotten about him. Then one day, little Bat came to Sabretooth with news that there was a small, pink baby in the cave now and that the Woman was very fond of him.

"*Just so,*" said Sabretooth, "*but what is it that the baby likes?*"

"*The little one likes things to play with, things that are soft and cuddly. He likes warm things to hold when he sleeps,*" Bat replied. Sabretooth thought then that his time had come and so he made his way back to the Cave. He hid nearby until Man, Booa and Vykr left to hunt for the day. Woman was busy cooking. The crying of the baby interrupted her work so she carried him to just outside the door of the cave and gave him a soft vykr hide ball to play with. Yet still the baby cried.

"Sabretooth chose this moment to make himself known. Approaching the child he reached out with a velveted paw and batted the baby gently on the cheeks. The baby cooed happily as Sabretooth rubbed against his chubby little legs. Hearing the baby's laughter, Woman smiled and came to the door to see what had caught the child's attention. When Woman saw Sabretooth, she angrily chased him away, but this set the baby to crying again.

"On and on the baby cried, until Woman was at her wit's end. Finally Sabretooth came back. From outside the cave he called to Woman. *"Bring the child back outside and bring with you a clay knob tied to a string and I will make your child laugh once more."*

"Woman did as the Sabretooth bid, for she could take the child's crying no longer and nothing she did had any effect. Tying a string around a small clay knob, she carried it outside along with the baby. Sabretooth bid her place the baby on the ground and drag the clay bauble around in the dirt. As she did so, Sabretooth chased the bauble, patting it with his paws, rolling head over heels with it and soon had the baby laughing once more. The baby chased after Sabretooth and together the two of them played until the baby was exhausted and curled up against his warm, furry sides. Sabretooth sang his own kind of Song to lull the baby to sleep, leaving Woman amazed.

"Very well, you who walk alone. Come and be welcome in our home, so long as you do as you have done today, for all time. You are quick and you are clever and for that you have my thanks. Come and go as you please, sleep by the warm fire, and tend the child gently when he cries," Woman said. Sabretooth eagerly agreed, for the warm fire was pleasing indeed.

"And even to this day, do the Plainsfolk keep the little sabreteeth among the *yerts,* for they do keep the children entertained and they will band together to drive away their cousins, the longteeth, should the great Plains hunters come calling at the herds or the camp. Yet still, the sabreteeth walk alone, coming and going as they please and calling no man 'Master'."

The children laughed and clapped at her story and she laughed with them, wondering what Aleister would have thought of her choice of story.

For the next half hour Kalla regaled the children with several more stories from all over the world of De Sikkari. By this time, more children, Pip included, and several adults had gathered around her, entranced. Even Aleister and the gamblers had wandered over.

"Hmm... we have, I think, time for just one more story before little heads should be laid to sleep. Big ones too, for that matter." A yawn accompanied the last.

"This last story is a personal favorite of mine. It begins long ago, in the province of Tishal, here on Argoth. It just so happened that in Tishal there lived a merchant who had made a vast fortune in trade. This merchant's name was Soren. It was autumn and Soren's wife left the skycity for the Plainsland, to visit family. Soren was very lonely. Days passed and the merchant grew ever more lonely. One beautiful autumn evening, while out on a stroll, he came upon a most lovely young maiden. Soren could no longer contain himself and he grabbed the young woman.

"*Who are you?*" Soren asked. The maiden smiled at him.

"*I am nobody, milord.*"

"*Well, then, Nobody, come away with me to my place,*" Soren said. At this the maiden tried to pull away, but Soren kept a firm grip on her.

"*Oh, no, milord. I couldn't do that.*"

"*Then where do you live, most beautiful one? I will go home with you!*" he replied.

"*Just over here, milord.*" She set off with Soren right beside her, keeping a good grip on her arm. It was not long before they arrived at a most wondrous house. What a surprise to find such a place nearby! Male and female servants clustered around to greet the young girl and it was only then that Soren realized that she was the daughter of the house.

Much to Soren's delight, the two slept together that night. In the morning a man whom Soren understood to be the girl's father came in.

"*You were meant to come here,*" the master of the house said, "*and now you must stay!*" The girl was ever so nice and Soren was so smitten with her that he soon forgot his wife. As for his house and children, he never gave them the first thought. He and the girl pledged eternal love to one another.

Meanwhile, Soren's family waited for him to return. At first they just assumed that he was out catting around, like usual, but when days passed and he never returned, they began to fear the worst. They searched and searched, but no trace of him could they find. During this time Soren became comfortably installed in his new home and before long his new wife was pregnant. After she had an easy delivery of a healthy baby boy, the two grew even closer. Time flew by and Soren had not a care in the world.

Back at his old home, his affluent brothers grew more and more worried. Search though they had, they had found no trace of Soren. They assumed he was dead, though they had not recovered a body. The brothers carved a statue of the god Carron Death-bringer, just the height of Soren. When the statue was completed they prostrated themselves before it, praying that they would find Soren's body.

Suddenly a man with a large stick arrived at Soren's new house. While the whole household fled in terror, the man poked Soren in the back with the stick and used it to force him through a tight passageway to the outside. This was the thirteenth day since Soren's disappearance. The family was outside before the statue, shaking their heads over what had happened. Imagine their surprise when a small, monkey-like creature crawled out from under a storage shed nearby! Through the jabber of astounded voices, one managed to break through.

"*It's me!*" Soren said. "*Don't you recognize me?*" Though they didn't recognize the man, they recognized the voice. His brothers drew him up onto the veranda and into the house. Soren explained how desperate he had been for female companionship, what with his wife gone away and all and how he had married the gentleman's daughter. He went on and on about his new family, bubbling with pride over his little son.

"*But where is he?*" the eldest brother asked. Soren pointed to the storage shed.

"*Why, right over there!*"

Soren's brothers exchanged looks. This was strange news. Soren looked terribly thin and sick. He still wore the clothes he had disappeared in, though now they were all dirty and disheveled. The brothers sent servants to check under the storehouse, where they found a passel of foxes. Their brother had been tricked by a *kitsune,* a fox spirit. He had married the fox spirit and was no longer in his right mind.

A Technomancer trained as an esper architect was sent for to try and purify his mind. It took the esper architect many a long day to break the spell over Soren, but the merchant finally returned to himself and was sorely embarrassed over the whole incident. The thirteen days he had spent under the storehouse had passed as thirteen years to Soren and the few inches between shed and ground had seemed a grand and stately mansion. Such is the power and the mischievousness of the fox-spirits. So remember, never get too greedy or be unfaithful, lest the foxes come to teach you a lesson!"

This last story elicited quite a bit of laughter and applause from the adults in the crowd. Belief in the fox-spirits and their pranks were quite prevalent among the Argosians. Kalla bowed to her audience and the crowd began to dissipate. She yawned as Aleister came up.

"Looks like we could both use some rest!" she said. He nodded agreement, trying, and failing, to stifle a yawn.

"Indeed. After you, milady," Aleister replied.

Master Wylsin was waiting for them by the stairs.

"Your rooms are on the upper level, last on the right. I hope you find everything satisfactory."

"If the beds are soft, I'll be happy." Aleister yawned again. Kalla gave the innkeeper a nod.

"I'm sure all will be fine. Dinner was wonderful, Master Wylsin." Kalla pulled another coin from thin air.

"I know the Empire will foot our bill, Master Innkeep, but I prefer to pay my own way. Save it for a special occasion," the mage said. Wylsin nodded as he pocketed the coin.

"You are too kind, Lady Mage, too kind. You are a credit to the Kanlon." His voice dropped, muttering darkly. "Unlike our last magi guest."

Kalla had started up the stairs, but she turned back.

"What was that? When was another mage here? What did they do to you?" she asked. Wylsin flashed her a sour look, at odds with his cheerful disposition.

"No offense, Lady Mage. It was two weeks ago. Another of the House Solidor came through. An arrogant male, tall, quite slender, with flaming red hair and icy blue eyes. One of the Wolf-folk I believe, though I've never seen one with red hair before. He scared the young ones so bad, I'm surprised they even approached you. Said it wasn't his place to provide 'common entertainment'. Said a great deal more too.

"But his magister, that man was enough to put fear in the Death-bringer Himself. Very cold, aloof. A towering giant of a man, with spiked plate armor, all in black. Never took it off. Insisted on standing guard all night outside the mage's door, he did. As if I would allow harm to come to any under my roof!"

With those descriptions the mage and magister could be none other than Vander kyl'Solidor and Shingar, two she knew well and avoided when possible. Vander had expressed an interest in her long ago and had not been pleased when she turned him down. The fiery-tressed mage had been cold and distant towards her after that. She shuddered. Even if she had been interested in Vander, knowing that Shingar would feel any passion shared gave her the shivers, though at the time Vander hadn't yet taken a magister. She wondered if it would have made a difference. Shingar was one reason she had never had any desire to take a magister. The man had been a rapist and a killer before Vander had chosen him. She made a face, shuddering again at the thought.

"I am sorry, Master Wylsin. I hope the encounter hasn't tainted the people too badly. Most magi are not nearly so... brusque. I can assure you, I feel quite safe here! My magister will stay nice and snug in his own room, won't you, Aleister?" Kalla said.

"Indeed I will, milady," Aleister replied with a grin. Wylsin returned it.

"Sleep well, Lady Mage, Magister," the innkeeper replied. Aleister nodded to the innkeep and started up the stairs, Kalla following behind. Her thoughts turned from Vander and Shingar to yet another complication she had often dwelt on. Mage and magister were tuned to one another's feelings. The bond was primarily empathic at the moment, though eventually they would be able to share coherent thoughts as well. Useful, but it meant that *all* emotions were shared.

She blushed without meaning to. That wasn't something she really need worry about. Most who had approached her with a romantic interest had been people seeking to get at her power, something she wasn't falling for.

It was a disturbing thought anyway, that a magister felt such from a mage. She found the reverse equally disturbing, but she could buff her shields enough to keep out such an unwanted intrusion should Aleister choose to find entertainment somewhere along the way.

Lost in thought, Kalla was unaware that said magister had stopped walking. She ran smack into the back of him.

"Oof," the mage grunted as she hit him. Aleistet whirled around, catching an arm to steady her. Kalla jerked away as if he'd burnt her, causing him to frown.

"Are you okay, milady?"

"Yes, I'm fine. Just tired. Guess I wasn't paying attention to where I was going."

Concern creased the magister's face and Kalla felt a tentative probe to her own mind. Alarmed at how swiftly Aleister was learning, she slammed her shields shut with enough force to cause him to wince, but not before she again caught the odd undercurrent in his emotions.

"Very well. Your room is here, looks like." Aleister held the door open for her. "Sure you don't want me to stand guard all night?" he asked, favoring her with another mischievous grin.

Kalla thought that was another reason he had the name 'Sky Fox', for fox he did look like when he grinned like that. She scowled.

"No, I want you to get some sleep so you aren't grumpy in the morning."

"I am *not* grumpy!" Aleister returned her scowl with one of his own.

"Yes, you are. And I'm going to get grumpy if I don't get to sleep.

Good night, Aleister."

"Good night." The Fox disappeared into his room and Kalla closed the door to her own. She slipped out of her robes and changed the baggy pants and tunic underneath for some more comfortable for sleeping. The clothes provided by the Imperials were an almost perfect fit. She wondered briefly if Aleister had fared so well. If not, she could alter them tomorrow.

The next several days passed much the same. Traveling filled the mage's days and storytelling her evenings. At every town, she heard news of Vander and Shingar and what she heard was not good. The Solidoran Mage had declined to help many who needed it. She knew that healing wasn't his strongest skill, but they were good enough to have helped at least a few of these people. Visits by magi were not that common, after all.

Kalla helped any who came seeking, spending quite a bit of time and energy in healing. She couldn't begrudge the people that. To her, helping and healing was the point and purpose of what being magi was all about. She found it a bit troublesome that Vander had refused help and resolved to bring the matter to the Sin' of Cryshal. It was a breach of Cryshal's unspoken contract with the people of Sikkari, if aid was refused for no good reason. One errant mage could cause a great deal of trouble for the Kanlon.

As they drew closer to the Deep Forest, the towns grew further and further apart, eventually disappearing for good. At the last town, Kalla stocked up on extra supplies for both the humans and the vykr. There was no telling how long they might have to wander the Forest before finding Gasta. If the Keeper did not want to be found, he would not be found and though she could weave edible food from nothingness, that took power she could little spare in the Forest.

Deep Forest, Argoth, Year of the Golden Hart, 2013 CE

On the eleventh day, they reached the Forest itself. Aleister's trepidation grew as they approached the massive forest with its monolithic trees. All week, as the forestlands grew thick about them, the magister had grown more and more uneasy. Though he had lost a fear of the sky, the Arkaddian still had a healthy fear of being hemmed in by trees.

Mage and magister stopped the vykr at the Forest entrance. Kalla took a deep breath, inhaling the rich smells of green, growing things. Scents of jasmine and thistlehart drifted on the air.

She drew in another breath and let it out in a long, ululating sound that rang through the trees. Aleister jumped, cursed his reaction.

"What in blazes was that for?"

"To let the guardians know we are here." Before she could say more, a call echoed back at them, first from one point, then another, then another.

"There. Now we have permission to enter. Stay to the path. This is important. You must keep to the path or you will become hopelessly lost. There are beings in the Forest that would take great delight in luring a human to their deaths in the trees. No matter what you think you see or hear, do not leave the path," Kalla said.

Aleister gave her a shaky nod.

"If it's so dangerous, should we be going in?" the magister asked.

"The Forest can be dangerous, kas, but only if you do not show it proper respect. However, this is where Gasta lives and if any can give us a good starting place, it will be the Keeper of the Forest." Kalla nudged her mount to a walk and started down the path, the Forest swallowing her like some great hungry beast. With some hesitation, Aleister followed.

The farther in they went, the darker it became, until the light vanished altogether. Kalla conjured magelight to light the way, the orbs glowing like tiny suns in the darkness. She could feel her magister getting more and more antsy, so she decided to halt for the night.

"Here's a good place to stop. We'll make camp and get some rest," she said.

"How can you tell it's night-time?" Aleister's voice sounded grateful.

"It is. Trust me." As he would figure out soon enough, day and night counted for nothing in the Forest. From here on out they would have to use magelight to show the way. Kalla fixed the orbs in place.

Aleister took the vykr over to a tree and tethered them, leaving the leads long. Kalla walked the area, pacing out a circle, letting Aleister's soft voice relax her even as it soothed the beasts. He unsaddled them, brushed their long, shaggy fur, checked their hooves and fed them, while Kalla walked the circle twice more, each time weaving a stronger shield.

By the time she was finished, her warding was strong enough to keep out all but Gasta himself, but it served another purpose as well. It kept them inside. Though Kalla knew she was strong enough to withstand the temptations beyond the path, she was not so sure about Aleister, especially in his current fretful state. Despite her reassurances, the gloomy forest still unsettled the Arkaddian.

Their tasks complete, they made camp- building a fire, collecting wood, putting dinner together, cleaning up- all in relative silence. Kalla wondered how long it would be before Aleister would go crazy in the quiet. Quiet didn't bother her. She enjoyed the Forest, having spent quite a bit of time in it when she was younger. Her father had brought her here as often as he could to teach her respect for the unknown, and to instill in her a certain degree of fearlessness. The pair were drowsing around the fire after dinner, when Aleister finally lost the battle. Kalla chuckled to herself, as his voice broke the silence.

"Milady, can I ask a question?"

"You can ask. I might not answer," she said.

"Fair enough. Lady, why did you choose me? Out of all the others? Surely there were better choices, yes?" Aleister asked.

"I've already told you, I wasn't looking for brute strength. Nor was I looking for someone who had truly been worthy of a death sentence." She shrugged. "Choosing you felt right. I knew you weren't a killer, by your own admission and by the truth-read. Help any?"

Aleister nodded slowly and Kalla again caught the strange undercurrent to his thoughts, tinged, oddly enough, with a bit of shame and fear. This time she felt him actively suppress it before she could focus on it. He was silent for a moment more.

"Another thing I've been meaning to ask- the coins you've given the stableboys and innkeepers, you made them from nothing. How?"

Kalla laughed softly.

"No, that was merely illusion, not magick. I am skilled enough to weave something from 'nothing', but the coins came from my own purse."

"But how is it possible to make something from nothing?" Aleister asked.

"I'm not sure I can explain it to one not a mage, but I'll try. There are tiny particles all around us. Everything, even the air itself, is made from these unseen particles. I'm not really pulling something from nothing, but reweaving the pattern of the particles. Not all magi are skilled in Alchemy, but it happens to be something I excel at," Kalla said.

Aleister shook his head. "I'm not sure I understand. If it can't be seen, how can you manipulate it?"

"I don't have to see it with my eyes. I see it in my mind. We see with magick's eyes."

Aleister shook his head, puzzlement drifting through the link. He opened his mouth to say something more, but an eerie howling rent the air, causing the Magister to jump. His eyes were wide in the firelight.

"What was that?" he asked, voice barely a whisper.

"*Cus silthair*, better known as sabre wolves. They won't bother us. The area is shielded and they will avoid the path," Kalla said. She noticed her magister squinting into the darkness beyond the shield. In the distance, pale balls of blueish light bobbed and wove, accompanied by eerie blue-green lights that winked off and on as they darted low to the ground.

"The blue, bobbing lights will be will-o-wisps. One reason you shouldn't leave the path. Follow one and you'll get lost and end up in the wolves' bellies. The others come from the wolves themselves," Kalla explained.

Aleister hugged himself, working to put a stranglehold on the fear he was feeling.

"Tell a story? Please? Anything to take my mind off of this place,"

he asked in a plaintive voice.

"Very well." Kalla relaxed, settling into her 'story mode'.

"Long ago, when the world was young and new, Bear had a long, beautiful tail. Bear was so proud of his long tail. He would go around asking everyone-

"*Don't you think my tail is the most beautiful you've ever seen?*"

And everyone agreed with Bear, but not because they truly liked his tail. They thought Bear very vain, but sharp claws and teeth make for pretty compliments. They all told Bear how much they loved and admired his fluffy, plush tail.

Now one day, during winter, Bear happened to come across Fox fishing in the ice. Fox was surrounded by a whole pile of delicious-looking fish and Bear decided he wanted some fish too. Fox knew that the prideful Bear was hungry and so he decided to play a trick on him, to teach a lesson. Bear ambled up to him and plopped down on the ice.

"*Hello, Brother Fox. Where did you get all of those tasty look-ing fish?*" Bear asked, mouth watering. Fox pointed to a hole in the ice.

"*I caught them, Brother Bear,*" Fox replied.

Bear gave Fox a puzzled look. "*But how, Brother Fox? You have nothing to fish with,*" he asked. Fox gave a sly grin.

"*Why I used my tail, Brother Bear. It's the best thing to fish with! Shall I show you how? Then you can have as many fish as you want.*"

"*Yes, please,*" Bear answered in his deep, gruff voice. He was so surprised. Using one's tail to fish? What a novel idea. Bear followed Fox to another part of the frozen lake and Fox showed him how to dig out a fishing hole.

"*Now put your long, beautiful tail in the water. Wait until you feel the fish bite it, then you can pull out your tail with the fish attached. But-*" Fox held up a cautionary paw, "*it is very important that you sit very still. Be patient and do not move or you will scare the fish away.*"

Bear nodded and put his tail in the water. He sat very still, waiting patiently. Time passed and Bear fell asleep, waiting for the fish to bite.

Meanwhile Fox had gathered his fish and returned home.

A few hours later Fox returned to the lake, to find Bear still asleep on the ice. His dark fur was white with snow. Fox chuckled to himself and snuck up behind Bear.

"*Bear, Bear! Wake up! I can see a fish on your tail!*"

Bear woke with a fright and felt a sting in his frozen tail.

"*I can feel it! I can feel it!*"

Bear jumped up, expecting to pull a fish out of the lake. Instead he snapped off his beautiful tail. Fox ran away laughing, while Bear bewailed the loss of his wonderful tail. That is why Bears today have only short, stubby tails.

So remember the lesson of Bear and Fox whenever you begin to become too prideful. Remember, too, that quite often cunning is better that brute strength any day!"

Aleister had grown more and more relaxed during Kalla's story and he was now so drowsy he was almost asleep. The magister stirred, and gratitude filtered through the bond, along with a faint echo of the unusual feeling that Kalla couldn't quite place.

"Thank you, milady. You must think me a fool for being scared of the Forest," he said.

"Not at all. Each of us carries our own fears, magi included," Kalla replied.

"What could you possibly be scared of? You don't seem afraid of anything," Aleister muttered sleepily.

"My fears are less tangible, but they are there. I just hide them well." Kalla sighed softly.

The Keeper of the Forest

Deep Forest, Argoth, Year of the Golden Hart, 2013 CE

They had been wandering the Forest for days now, going in circles and still they had not found the Keeper. The pair had set camp earlier, both dejected by their lack of success. Though it had become a habit for Kalla to tell a story before bed, this night neither were in the mood, and they surrendered to sleep earlier than usual.

Aleister jolted awake, the fine hairs along the back of his neck standing at attention. He glanced around, nervously searching the shield perimeter. As his eyes adjusted he found himself staring into a nightmare face. Glowing eyes barely illuminated a broad, heavy muzzle, topped by a slender, curved blade of bone. He panicked, reaching out to shake Kalla awake.

His touch triggered a fearsome reaction.

The sleeping mage grabbed the front of Aleister's shirt, jerking him down and rolling over to pin him to the ground. In her other hand a short blade glittered in the dim firelight. Aleister yelped, grabbing her hand before she could drive the blade home.

"It's me! Kalla, it's Aleister!" the magister yelled. Though her eyes were open they held no recognition. They were empty and cold as a bleak winter evening, as if no one were home inside.

He shuddered, still fighting for control of the blade. To be so small, the mage had great strength. Whether she sensed his fear or heard his words, life slowly returned to her face. She relaxed, lowering the blade.

"Yesss?" Kalla's voice was calm as she pushed away from him, the blade disappearing back to wherever she'd pulled it from. He scrambled away, keeping a wary eye on her.

"What... what was that all about? Why'd you try to kill me?" Aleister swallowed hard, trying to calm his hammering heart.

"Why'd you try to wake me up? Don't you remember me telling you that would be inadvisable?" Indeed, he dimly recalled that warning. He pointed to the shield, still shaky from the encounter. The sabre wolf was still there, pressed against the side. As the Mage turned her attention to it, the bone blade on its muzzle ignited with an eldritch glow. It blinked at her.

Follow. She heard the words without hearing them. From his expression, so did the magister.

"It wants us to follow it?" he asked. Kalla nodded. They quickly packed up and saddled the vykr, while the wolf waited patiently outside the shield. When Kalla dropped it, the creature moved off, heading into the forest. The mage followed without pause, leaving Aleister scrambling to catch up.

"Milady, would you have really killed me?" Aleister asked in a soft lilting voice fraught with uncertainty. Kalla shifted slightly in her saddle.

"Maybe, maybe not. I *did* warn you." She did not speak for a long moment. "That is one reason why I never wanted to take a magister. I can protect myself. It's also earned me a nickname-Wolf that Sleeps. A lone frost wolf reacts the same way if disturbed while asleep," she said. He gave a shaky laugh.

"Wolf that Sleeps, indeed."

"I am sorry, Aleister. Kill you I might have, but I would have regretted it when I came to my senses. I like having you around." Kalla turned her focus to the sabre wolf loping along ahead of them. A moment later, Aleister tensed when he realized that they were surrounded by sabre wolves. All around them, blades glowed with eldritch light.

"Where are they taking us?" the magister asked.

"To Gasta. Any of the Forest's creatures can serve as his Voice when he wants. So long as they are under the Keeper's control, we will not be harmed," she replied. His thoughts said he didn't believe her, but before he could give voice to his concerns they broke through the trees, into an open glen. An odd tumble of boulders was the only thing within. The wolves stopped just outside the clearing, keeping to the woods. Kalla rode forth, giving Aleister no choice but to follow. He kept looking at the boulders.

"Those look like an animal… a big, slinky animal." As if in response to his words, the ground rumbled and the 'boulders' shifted and melted away, to reveal the presence of a very real Gasta. The Keeper was huge and when he rose to his feet, he towered over the two humans. Fine white fur covered a muscular body. Tufted ears twitched as the slender head dipped down. Warm amber eyes full of wisdom regarded them with a slightly amused expression.

Grove of Gasta, Deep Forest, Argoth, Year of the Golden Hart, 2013 CE

What do you seek in my Forest, little Wolf? It has been a long time since you were last here. Gasta said.

Kalla dismounted, kneeling before the great creature. Aleister followed suit.

"We seek answers, Great One and I knew that if any could help, it would be you," the mage said respectively. A dry chuckle filled their minds.

What answers would you have of me? Gasta's voice was a soft rumble in their minds. Kalla settled down before the Keeper.

"I believe the Nagali is waking, Great One," Kalla replied.

What makes you think this?

"Skycities and ground cities all over De Sikkari have been attacked by creatures enslaved for that purpose. Even Argoth was attacked, though the Empire's ships kept the attackers at bay. The creatures had been impaled with poison spikes." Kalla gestured to Aleister, where he had pulled a slim package from his pack. He carefully unwrapped the many layers protecting the spike that they had taken from Amaterasu. Gasta brought his head closer to the spike, sniffing it. Reaching out with a claw, he gingerly rolled it around.

This is kepfal, *a very dangerous drug that requires extensive knowledge to cultivate. I had thought the knowledge of its manufacture long since lost. I will take this. It should be destroyed.*

Kalla nodded and Aleister carefully rolled the spike back up and placed it before the Keeper.

"That is not all, Great One. The day after Cove Rock attacked Sevfahl, Amaterasu and I did a fire scrying." She went on to describe all that she and the wyvern had seen. The Keeper rumbled unhappily, tail twitching like an angry cat.

This is not good news. The seal should not have broken. You will have to recreate the binding, if you be up to the task. The Quill you need first. It can be found in the vaults of Araun, Lord of Xibalba. Gasta said.

Kalla frowned. "How do we reach Xibalba, Great One?"

There are many portals to Xibalba, little Wolf. They are scattered all across De Sikkari. From Argoth, the closest lie in Evalyce. The strongest known portal lies within the borders of Arkaddia.

But the trials of the Underworld are many. You must be sure you are prepared to face Araun and his guardians before you venture there.

Kalla nodded. "And of the Elephant Lord?"

I am sorry, little Wolf. I do not know where the Elephant Lord dwells. Amber eyes regarded Aleister.

Seek the Temple of Inari. It lies farther within, at the center of the Forest. My wolves will lead you there.

"We will find more answers there?" Kalla asked. Beside her Aleister fidgeted, clearly uneasy at going deeper into the Forest. Gasta's lips wrinkled, pulling back to expose sharp fangs as he laughed.

You will find what you need, not necessarily what you want. It would behoove you to go to the Temple before approaching Araun. Sleep now. My wolves will guard you. When you wake they will guide you to the Temple.

Gasta blew out a long breathe that washed over them with a scent of honeysuckle. In unison Kalla and Aleister slumped over, asleep before they hit the ground. Gasta gave them one last, penetrating look before disappearing into the Forest. He needed to have a talk with the King of Foxes before the pair managed to reach the Temple.

* * *

Kalla woke abruptly. All around the grove, eldritch lights glittered as sabre wolves flitted through the trees, but the Keeper was nowhere to be seen. She realized with a start that she had been sleeping with her head resting against Aleister's shoulder. For his part, her magister was still sound asleep. She covered her eyes with a hand. Great Balgeras. Gasta's enchanted sleep must have kept both of them still while they slept. She shuddered to think what would have happened if Aleister had shifted even a bit. In his sleep, he might be dead before she realized it was him. Then again, maybe not. She might have unconsciously realized she'd fallen asleep near him. The few times she'd ever fallen asleep near those she didn't consider a threat, the reaction hadn't been triggered if they woke her.

The mage knew she should get up, should wake him so that they could get to the Temple of Inari, but she didn't want to. She was content to stay where she was, listening to Aleister's rhythmic breathing. Beneath that, she could hear the slow, steady beat of his heart. Kalla marveled yet again at the simple magick that was life itself. What but the One could have created such a wonder? As a Healer, Kalla knew all of the intricacies of the body and still she was amazed at the fluidity of function.

She sighed, letting the sound of heart and breath lull her nearly back to sleep. She pondered over Gasta's advice to seek the Temple of Inari. Inari was the father of the forest *kitsune,* the fox spirits of Argosian legend. She remembered hearing tales of the Temple hidden in the Forest, but she'd never been to it, nor even seen it despite her many excursions into the Forest. Kalla's eyes drifted closed, drawing her back into sleep.

Aleister woke, stifling a yawn, then froze when he realized that Kalla was curled up beside him, head resting on his shoulder. He frowned, giving the sleeping mage a sidelong glance. Since he didn't want to risk gaining closer acquaintance with the hidden knife she bore, Aleister decided to be patient and wait for her to wake rather than wake her himself.

He closed his eyes, listening to the sounds of the forest. Despite the danger, he found comfort in the mage's presence. Kalla had given him a new lease on life, doing more for him than any other, save the Argosian with whom he'd spent a great deal of his life. Melaric Wolffsson had treated Aleister as a son, giving him the comfort of a family and the benefit of fatherly guidance during a time in his life when he could have gone seriously astray. He remembered Kalla's comment regarding her cavalier attitude in regards to her own life and well-being. Aleister knew what it was like to not have anyone care if you lived or died. His own life had pretty much been like that since Melaric had passed away. He only hoped he could live up to her expectations.

Kalla blinked, going very still. She hadn't intended to fall asleep again, yet that is exactly what she'd done. Something was different now and the difference had woken her.

"Good... morning, milady. I wondered how long I might have to stay still before you woke. I didn't want a repeat of last night." Her magister's voice was light, but there was a hint of reproach in his thoughts. The odd emotion chased after it, disappearing before she could catch it. She stirred and sat up, yawning.

"My apologies, Aleister." She ran her fingers through her hair. "I... uh... meant to move earlier, when you were still sleeping. Guess I fell back asleep," she said.

"No apologies needed, milady. As long as you don't try to kill me again!" He stood and stretched, glancing around the clearing. Their vykr stood placidly nearby, apparently not bothered by the wolves that still haunted the woods about them. Aleister snagged a pack. "I'm guessing you want a cold breakfast, so we can get moving, yes?" he asked with a slight grin. She nodded, conjuring balls of magelight to aid him as he poked around in the pack and pulled out a loaf of brown bread and a half a wheel of hard, yellow cheese. The Sky Fox broke them in half, passing part to Kalla. They ate quickly and mounted their vykr. Kalla conjured more magelight globes and fixed one to Aleister's essence, ensuring that it would stay with him. The others she left free. Since she had conjured them, they would follow her anyway. As if by some unseen signal, a wolf entered the clearing, coming to a halt before them.

Follow. The command in the unheard voice was clear and Kalla nudged her mount into an easy trot. Behind her, she heard Aleister murmuring softy to his vykr. As they rode, Kalla noticed that the trees grew ever larger. At the center of the forest, the massive trees were so big that it would have taken several people to come close to circling one with outstretched arms. Their branches soared overhead, forming a graceful, vaulting arch of emerald high above the Temple that stood in the clearing. Weathered blocks of stone told the tale of the Temple. Vines covered most of the building, obscuring the true size of it.

The Temple doors were likewise covered, as were the two immense stone foxes guarding the entrance. On the far side of the clearing a small brook bubbled merrily. The sabre wolves melted back into the forest and Kalla sent a silent thanks to Gasta for their aid. Mage and magister dismounted and tethered the vykr near the brook, leaving the leads long. There was no telling how long they would be inside the Temple, so Aleister provided them with what he hoped would be ample food. Unlike Rang'Moori horses, the Arkaddian vykrs weren't prone to overeating. There was little danger they would eat all of the food in, say, a day and the Magister had left enough food for several days.

The pair shouldered their packs and moved to the entrance. Aleister tugged the vines loose from one great wooden door. Beneath, he found a massive brass ring. He pulled, putting all of his effort into it. With a groan, the door swung open, leaving a gaping black hole behind. The magister sidled through the door first, wary of hidden traps and dangers. The light globe bobbing above him illuminated a long dark corridor. He took a few more steps into the gloom. Working with Melaric, he'd been in his fair share of ruins such as these and one never knew what might be waiting. A wave of anger hit him and he spun around, wondering what had made the mage so upset. He was greeted by a blank stone wall. The door was gone and Kalla was nowhere in sight. He pushed against the wall, thinking it an illusion, but his fingers touched cold stone. Well now. This was a nice predicament. Aleister weighed his options. He could wait here and see if Kalla showed up or he could find another way out. He decided to seek another path. He didn't know how he'd ended up here, but if the mage wasn't with him now, she likely wasn't going to show up later.

The Temple of Inari

Aleister set off down the corridor, thankful for the magelight that Kalla had tagged to him, since he didn't have a torch handy. Keeping a watchful eye out for traps and other hidden dangers, he followed the path until he came to an intersection. Trusting in the instincts that had made him such a good thief, Aleister headed down the left-hand path. Several intersections and an uneventful thirty minutes later (save for the simmering anger from his still absent mage), he was stopped by what appeared to be a dead end. A pair of giant stone frogs flanked the corners of the blank wall.

The Arkaddian frowned. The statues looked like the smaller stone frogs known as 'prosperity toads' to the Argosians. Melaric had kept one. But these frogs didn't have the coins in their mouths common to the smaller ones. He leaned closer, running his hands over one of the stone frogs. There was a groove in the mouth, as if disks might have once been there. On a whim he reached into his coin pouch and fished two coins out. At the very least he could leave an offering in the hopes he might find a way out. He pushed a copper coin into the mouth of first one frog, then the other. As the second coin slid home, the ground rumbled and the 'wall' before him slid up, revealing the continuation to his path. Beyond lay a vast room, barely illuminated by the ball of magelight. Water trickled in the distance. As he stepped into the room, the door slid shut behind him, sealing the exit off.

Kalla snarled angrily, pacing around in tight circles before the doors to the Temple of Inari. Though she had been right behind Aleister when he'd entered, she had found herself back outside. Each and every attempt she had made to enter the Temple resulted in her being cast back outside the doors.

Likewise, her attempts to teleport to Aleister met with the same misfortune. The Temple would not let her enter and she'd drained a great deal of energy trying to reach her magister. Through the bond she could feel that he was a bit anxious, but other than that, his mind was occupied. A few times alarm shot through the bond, never lasting very long.

Kalla sighed as her stomach growled. The mage had been pacing outside the doors for several hours and her body was letting her know she needed to eat and to rest. Grudgingly she set a camp near the Temple, fixing a simple soup for dinner. Afterwards, she drowsed near the fire, wondering how she was going to get to Aleister. As she thought of him, a feeling of loneliness filtered through the bond. Wherever he was, she could tell he had at least eaten and that he was tired and grumpy now.

Aleister sighed and trudged his way down yet another dark corridor. From the vault of the stone frogs he'd had only one option to leave. He'd taken it and followed his previous habit of taking every left turn he'd come across. There had been a few traps along the way, but those he avoided easily. More stone frog doors had taken more of his coin, yet he was still trapped in the Temple.

He'd been here for several days and his food was running low. He felt sure his bones would end up gracing the Temple in a tribute to a treasure hunter's folly. He wondered where Kalla was and if she would be affected by his death. He could still feel her, though the bond seemed to be getting weaker. She was tired, angry and frustrated. Aleister came to a halt before another blank wall guarded by stone frogs. He grimaced as he fished the last two coins out of his pouch. Shrugging, he shoved the coins in the frogs' mouths. The door rumbled open and he stepped through.

Kalla sank to the ground in frustration. She had spent the previous day making her way around the Temple, trying to find another way in, but the only entrance to be found was the one Aleister had gone through. She bit her lip with worry. He had grown more and more dejected over the last two days. She sensed that he'd given up hope of getting out. More disturbing was the fact that the bond between them seemed to be getting fainter, which could only mean they were separated by a great distance. She perked up as a sense of sudden fear came through the bond. It faded, to be replaced later by an intense sadness, leaving the Mage wondering what her Magister was going through.

Aleister gasped as his heart leapt to his throat. Each stone frog door had led to a vaulted room and this one was no exception. The air in this room was warmer than the rest of the Temple. At the far side of the room a form moved, shrouded in darkness. Aleister took a step forward and the magelight illuminated what looked to be a pair of giant paws. The paws shifted and nails scraped stone as the huge creature stood. It advanced and the magister retreated until his back hit the smooth stone wall. He swallowed hard as the figure came into view of the bobbing magelight. A giant fox, black as midnight, sporting nine fluffy brushes. He laughed weakly.

"Inari, I presume?"

The figure regarded him for a moment, a sly grin upon its furry face.

Indeed. Welcome home, child. The Fox King's voice was warm in his mind.

Aleister tilted his head, brows furrowed.

"Home? I don't understand. Argoth is not my home..."

Inari regarded him for a moment before turning away and striding off into the darkness.

Follow me, little Fox.

Nervously, the magister followed the Fox King through the room. They went down a short corridor and into an open courtyard within the Temple. Moonlight glittered on a pool of water in the center. Aleister looked up and saw the sky for the first time in days upon days, stars spangling the inky expanse like diamond dust. He nearly wept for the sight of the open sky instead of the trees that had shadowed them all this time. Inari stopped before the pool.

Gasta has told me of the Nagali's awakening. I can give you no answers to help you in your search, but I can, perhaps, give you something that you will find useful. Look into the pool, my child.

Aleister came up beside the Fox King and knelt before the pool. At first he merely saw his reflection staring back at him. The King of Foxes touched a paw to the still waters and the scene shifted. He saw a great frost wolf, the grizzled and scarred alpha of a pack. The scene dissolved into a vixen trapped in a bear trap. The trapped fox spirit begged a hunter not to kill her. In return she offered him her heart.

A ripple and the *kitsune* was gone. He saw a family in Kymru. The father, a sheepherder. The mother, a well-beloved herbalist. A young boy took great pride in helping his father with the herds. An older girl helped the mother make her rounds and tend the house. The entire family seemed the height of happiness.

Another ripple and the family was engulfed by scenes of an Argosian captain and his gunner, a scene flashing by that looked eerily familiar. In the end, the ship was destroyed, both captain and gunner lost. The style of ship was some 150 years out of date. The fireball of the ship's destruction led to scenes of an Arkaddian war party, in the time when the great Arkaddian Empire was just being forged. The vykr warriors were at the van of the great Khan Arkaddia's army. He saw the conquests of his ancestors through two of the vykr warriors' eyes. The warriors became generals in the army and went on to die of old age, well respected. These faded into scenes of a merchant family in Ishkar. Husband and wife ran a small textile shop in the city of Calderi. This family, like the one in Kymru, were happy and content.

The scene shifted again and Aleister gasped for what he saw was Melaric, when the Argosian was much younger. A beautiful young wife succumbed to childbirth. Though mother died, the child survived and the father doted upon her. The child grew and father and daughter traveled the length and breadth of Argoth, spending much time in the Forest.

The young child lived with her father on various military outposts. In several scenes Aleister recognized the Admiral from the *Kujata*. As she grew, he taught her to fly his ship. By the time she was ten she could fly the ship as well as her father. One day a pair of magi came to the outpost where father and daughter lived. They tested the girl-child and found her to have the gift of magick in her blood. They took her away and left the father both full of pride and grief.

Realization dawned on the magister- Kalla was the child taken from Melaric. Now he knew why she looked somewhat familiar. Melaric had kept a picture of himself and his young daughter.

The Argosian had never shared the story and Aleister had never pressed him on his past.

The waters rippled again and the Arkaddian saw scenes from his own past. He tried to turn away from the painful memories, but found his gaze locked on the pool. He saw his mother and a much younger version of himself subject to an abusive husband and father. He grew older and the abuse got worse. In a fit of rage, husband killed wife. In revenge a young son killed his father and fled, for patricide was a crime punishable by death no matter what the cause. Lost and alone, the young boy was taken in by an elderly Argosian thief who happened to be wandering Arkaddia. For many years Arkaddian and Argosian roamed the lands of Evalyce and the surrounding skycities, treasure hunting in ruins and finding bigger and better tests for their thieving skills. The Argosian became ill and in the end passed away. His young apprentice cremated his body, casting the ashes to the winds in honor of Argosian practices. The boy grew to man, surviving daring exploit after daring exploit until one day the fox was trapped and sentenced to execution. The last scene before the waters turned black was of Kalla approaching him in the depths of the Inferno.

Aleister felt tears on his cheeks and wiped a hand across his face. He looked up at Inari.

"I am sorry, King of Foxes. I don't understand. All except for the fact that Kalla is the child Melaric lost. And my own past..." Aleister said sadly. Inari chuffed softly.

No matter. You will understand in time. I will grant you the form that truly belongs to you, my child. I will also grant you proper weaponry, for your role as magister.

Aleister yelped as he felt a tingling sensation running through his skin. A pair of slender, long-bladed daggers materialized in his hands, almost as long as a vykr warrior's blades.

Very good, little Fox. Now will the weapons to change. Aleister frowned in concentration and the daggers became a vykr warrior's blades in truth.

You may make them whatever you wish them to be. If you wish them gone, simply will them to be gone. Aleister followed the Fox King's advice and concentrated. With the same tingling sensation, the blades disappeared.

"I thank you for the fine gift, Fox King. I pray I am worthy of such."

If I did not think so, I would not have offered it. It will help you in the coming days, of that I have no doubt. As for the form that truly belongs to you...

Inari bent down, touching his nose to Aleister's forehead. The Sky Fox sank to his knees, dizziness gripping him. He felt his bones shifting, though no pain came from it, and his world seemed to shrink and get smaller. Aleister held his hands up, only to find they were no longer hands but paws.

Fear thrilled through him and he turned to look over his shoulder. He was graced with a back covered in reddish-brown fur. Three plush fox brushes gave a weak wag. He opened his mouth to speak, but only a yip came out. Dry laughter filled his mind.

Do as with the weapons. Simply will yourself back.

The magister turned all his attention to returning to normal and with the same odd sensation of bones shifting he found himself back in his 'normal' form.

"Why do you say this is the form that truly belongs to me, Fox King?" Aleister asked.

It is the form of your soul, thus it is your true form. You will find it useful, never doubt that! You do not have all of the powers of a kitsune, *yet, but you will find those you do have useful as well. If things progress as they should, you will regain all of your rightful power.*

Now, I will return you to your mage before she brings the very stones of the Temple down on my head.

Amusement filled Aleister's mind as the room spun around him. He closed his eyes tightly against the disorienting sensation. A weight slammed into him and his eyes flew open to find the mage wrapping him in a hug. He returned it with some uncertainty.

"You're back! I was beginning to think I wouldn't see you again! The Temple wouldn't let me through. I've been trying for the past two days, but nothing I did worked," Kalla said.

"You... Wait, two days? I was in there for a week at least! I'm out of food and out of coin," the Sky Fox said ruefully. Kalla's brows drew down.

"How are you out of coin...? Food I can understand, but what did you spend coin on?" she asked. He made a face.

"I was feeding frogs," he replied, deadpan. This earned another puzzled look and he felt a gentle probe to his mind, testing his sanity.

"Okay... I'm not asking... The Temple is most likely in a small pocket dimension. The *kitsune* can manipulate time in such ways. That might also explain why the bond between us grew weaker," Kalla said. Aleister shrugged.

"I'm just glad to be out of there. I did manage to meet Inari, in the end. Unfortunately, he could not provide answers in aid of our quest.

"However, you'll be happy to know I now have proper weapons, courtesy of the Fox King." He concentrated and the magickal daggers shimmered into existence. He shifted them through several different forms for her. She nodded approval.

"Well, now. That's certainly a useful gift," Kalla murmured. Aleister grinned, happy that she was pleased and let the armor disappear.

"I gained more than that from the Fox King." He concentrated again and, with the painless shifting of bone, slipped into the fox form. Kalla's eyes widened and she took an involuntary step back. The fox's ears wilted and he changed back, unhappy and confused by her reaction. Aleister took a step towards her and Kalla stepped back, keeping away from him.

"You are *kitsune*," Kalla whispered, burying her face in her hands. "Great Balgeras, I have enslaved one of the fox kin."

"Enslaved?"

"You cannot tell me that being a magister is not a form of enslavement, Aleister, even if it did spare your life. If Inari granted you that form, it means that you were born with it," she said softly.

"I don't consider it being enslaved. I consider it an honor. And I was born Arkaddian. I know nothing of the fox spirits," Aleister protested. The mage shook her head sadly.

"In this lifetime you are Arkaddian, but your soul has lived many lifetimes. You began your very existence in this world as one of Inari's children," Kalla said softly. Aleister shook his head.

"I don't buy into all of that past life stuff. I was born Arkaddian and I will-"

"And you will die as more than Arkaddian, Sky Fox." Kalla gave a bitter laugh. "Your name is even more appropriate than you know.

"Sky Fox, if I could free you I would, but only death can sever the bond between mage and magister. Even the greatest of those at the Kanlon cannot undo it."

"But… but I don't want it undone. Unless you really do regret the choice…" His voice trailed off unhappily. Aleister had thought she would like the Fox King's changes. He hadn't counted on this reaction.

"No, I don't regret my choices at that time, but I do regret that I now have one of the fox kin bound to me. By now you should realize the regard in which we hold *kitsune*," Kalla said.

"I thought it would make you proud to be guarded by one, not make you dislike me," the magister replied.

"Oh, Aleister, I don't dislike you. I guess I just..." Whatever she was about to say was lost as growling filled the air. All around them bone blades ignited and wolves poured into the clearing. The vykr screamed as the sabre wolves tore into them and Aleister's alarm filled the link as the mage tried to process what was happening. There was no way they could fight the wolves and no way they could find their way out of the Forest alone. In a desperate attempt to save both their lives Kalla grabbed a handful of Aleister's shirt and willed herself back to the *Stymphalian.* Even the nearest town was incredibly far away. Teleporting to the airship would be no more dangerous than attempting the nearest town. Either could get them just as dead for the trying. Kalla's world went dark as she slammed into the pavement. Before she lost all consciousness she heard Amaterasu's alarmed roar and knew she had at least succeeded in getting them back to the ship.

Deep Forest, Skycity Argoth, Year of the Golden Hart, 2013 CE

In the dark depths of the Deep Forest, the young man collapsed to the ground, shaking with sobs, horror-stricken at what he'd done. The cold voice had been right. The Forest Lord had fallen easily when attacked by the dark magick that it had placed within him. The magick had petrified Gasta, turning the regal guardian to ivory. Even as the magick had overcome him, the Forest Lord had forgiven the man and it was that, perhaps, that hurt the worst.

As the guardian's transformation was complete, the young man had felt the geis on the creatures of the Forest lift. The sabre-wolves and other creatures were now free of Gasta's influence. Blades ignited as wolves gathered in the forest around him. He waited patiently, resigned to his fate. As the wolves closed in, the cold voice returned. It was pleased. He had done well.

The voice slithered through his mind, telling him how to focus his own power in order to teleport to safety. It was dangerous still, but perhaps he would survive. After all, he was still useful at the moment.

The voice also gave him new instructions, harder than even the last. He was to return to his Master and await the arrival of Kalla kyl'Solidor and her little fox and dispose of them, for they were becoming troublesome. His Master would bring them to him. The man tried to refuse, for he knew the mage and she had once, long ago, done him a great kindness. The cool voice expressed its disapproval. He would be the one to take care of the mage or he would pay the price. There would be no argument. He acquiesced, once more channeling his fear and unhappiness into more sustaining anger and bitterness. An omega wolf had no choice but to bow to those stronger.

Skycity Argoth, 10000 ft. above the Aeryth Ocean, Year of the Golden Hart, 2013 CE

The first thing Kalla became aware of was Aleister's gnawing anxiety. She heard his footsteps on the stairs as he realized she was awake. Relief flooded his face when he saw her.

"I didn't think you were going to wake up. You've been unconscious for three days. Of course, I was asleep for two of those as well," he said.

"… three days…" Kalla cringed at how weak her voice sounded. She struggled to sit up and found she was too weak to do even that. Giving up, Kalla sank back into the hammock. Aleister disappeared, returning with a welcome glass of water. She took the cup gratefully, savoring the coolness of it.

"Milady, why did the wolves attack us?"

"It means that Gasta no longer protects the Forest," the Mage murmured faintly.

"No longer protects the Forest?" the Magister asked.

"He is gone. The Keeper is dead..." Kalla's voice was soft, sad.

"I don't understand, milady. How can the Keeper be dead? What can kill such a being?"

"Gasta and Inari are spirits of place. They are demi-deities in their own right, but even they can be brought down, just like Al'dhumarna. As to exactly how, I have no idea..." The mage's voice trailed off as her strength faltered. Her eyes fluttered shut and she fell back into a more natural sleep.

Aleister watched her for a moment more before going back outside, where he was assaulted by an impatient wyvern. He assured Amaterasu that the mage was doing well, then went in search of the Outpost's Commander. Someone should know what Kalla had said regarding the Keeper. He didn't know if the wolves would keep to the Forest without Gasta.

Night-time found Aleister draped in the gunner's chair, rolling a small crystal orb across his knuckles. The orb had appeared the night before, when he was fretting over the Mage's condition. He wasn't completely sure, but he thought the orb was his 'fox-ball'. All *kitsune* had them, so he had learned from the Argosian soldiers. He hadn't told them he was one, not after Kalla's reaction. Just inquired into legends surrounding them. Part of a *kitsune's* soul were stored in the orbs. Aleister wished he could stuff all of his unhappiness and uncertainty into his, but it didn't seem to work that way. Right now he wasn't sure exactly what part of himself resided in his fox-ball. The orb itself gave off a multi-hued light. As with the armor and the fox form, he could now summon the orb whenever he wished, which was often. He found it relaxing. The magister had also been exploring other abilities he had gained, using insights drawn from the Argosian legends. So far he had managed to conjure green fox-fire and to craft simple illusions, more tricks in a *kitsune's* arsenal.

* * *

"Kalla."

"Kalla kyl'Solidor"

"Kalla kyl'Solidor!"

Kalla groaned at the insistent mental call. "What?" she replied in a groggy voice.

"Kalla kyl'Solidor!"

Her eyes snapped open as she recognized the voice in her mind as that of Grosso tem'Solidor, Master of House Solidor. The Masters of the Houses, due to their position, had the ability to mindspeak with any member of their House, no matter the distance.

"Yes, Master tem'Solidor?" Kalla asked in a subdued voice. There was a mental grunt as if the unseen speaker were satisfied that she was now listening properly.

"You have done as you were bid? You have found a magister?"

"Yes, Master tem'Solidor. I found a worthy magister on Sevfahl," she replied.

"If you found your magister on Sevfahl, why are you on Argoth? Were you not ordered to return home to begin your training once a magister was chosen?" The voice was stern and disapproving.

"Yes, Master tem'Solidor, but events at the Inferno made a trip to Argoth necessary." She went on to explain all that had happened.

"I see. No matter. You will report to Cryshal Kanlon. I expect you home in two days, Kalla kyl'Solidor. Do not disappoint me."

Grosso's gruff voice vanished as the connection broke. Kalla grimaced. She had no wish to return to Cryshal when there was so much that needed to be done. Grosso had sounded disbelieving of her story, that much had been plain.

The mage rose on shaky legs and made her way into the small bathroom. She turned on the shower and stepped inside, sighing as the hot water sluiced four days of sleep from her skin as she pondered Grosso's order. While she knew she would be better served by learning how to work more efficiently with Aleister, she chafed at the thought of doing nothing to stop the Nagali during the who knew how many weeks of training. Neither had she come to grips with the fact that her magister was *kitsune.*

Recalling his hurt look at her reaction made her feel terrible. It wasn't his fault and truly, what better magister for an Argosian?

She finished her shower and wandered to the front of the ship, wondering where said magister might be and finding him sound asleep in the captain's chair. Kalla wandered back to the kitchen area to fix something to eat. Now that she was up and moving around her tummy was rumbling angrily for lack of food during her four day fast.

The smell of breakfast was enough of a lure to rouse the Sky Fox and lure him back to the living quarters. He hesitated in the doorway, unsure of what welcome he might find there. Kalla turned around, favoring him with a grin and a plate of Argosian spiced potatoes, eggs, sausage and brown bread. He took the plate with a murmur of thanks and wedged himself in a space at the tiny table. Kalla had already eaten and she turned back to cleaning up the dishes. When she was finished, she came to sit at the table with him.

"We need to talk, Aleister. First, I want to apologize for my reaction. Please, don't think I dislike you. That's not the case and I've realized that Inari would not have made such a change if he disapproved of your being a magister. I am not one to override the Fox King's wishes," she said gently. He felt wary of her words, mentally tensed for a 'but' statement that never came.

"Thank you, milady. I hope I can still live up to your expectations," he said, his lilting voice soft and uncertain. Kalla sighed.

"You are doing just fine. Please, forgive me for upsetting you. I told you before, I felt I had chosen right and I still do."

"I forgive you." He gave her a sad smile. "And what is the second thing?"

"Second thing…? Oh, yes." She made a sour face. "We've been summoned to the Kanlon. Master tem'Solidor expects us in two days at the latest. We'll need to leave soon in order to make that deadline." Clearly the Mage was not happy with her new orders.

"Well, the ship is fully stocked and fueled. If we leave now we can reach Skycity Zinlin by nightfall and from there cover the rest of the distance to Cryshal tomorrow," Aleister said.

"That sounds like a good plan," Kalla replied. She stood and stretched, scooping up the empty plate. A brief thought and it was sparkling clean. From her magister she still got feelings of unhappiness and beneath that the lingering odd emotion that she still couldn't place. He ducked out of the kitchen area and made his way to the doors, Kalla right behind. When the mage stepped out of the ship, she was immediately enveloped in a red haze as Amaterasu pounced, using her wings to draw the Mage close.

You are well, Lady Mage? The wyvern's smoky breath washed over her. Kalla reached out and returned the wyvern's hug.

"I am well, my friend. How have they treated you? Good, I trust."

Oh, quite well, Lady Mage. They have let me hunt. I have watched the metal bird and kept it safe for you.

"Thank you, Amaterasu," Kalla said. The wyvern unfurled her wings and Kalla could see Aleister across the paddocks, speaking to the soldiers, most likely seeking permission to leave. He started back to the ship, with a wave to the soldiers behind.

"We have permission to leave now, if it please you, milady. A small escort will led us back to the boundary," he said. Kalla nodded, turning back to the wyvern.

"We might as well get going then. Amaterasu, we must go to Cryshal for some time. We must be trained to work well together, Aleister and I. Will you come with us?" she asked. A fierce orange eye regarded her.

If I will be allowed at Cryshal, then I will follow.

"The Kanlon should have no objections. They know now that a wyvern travels in my company," the mage replied.

Then I will go. You will learn and then we can go seek the feather.

"Very well, let's get going." Kalla followed Aleister back up the stairs and into the cabin. She expected him to take the captain's chair, but he turned to her instead.

"This chair is rightfully yours," he said quietly. She gave him a look and let her puzzlement filter through.

"The *Stymphalian* belongs to you, Aleister. You are her captain," she replied. He shook his head and gestured again for her to take the chair, refusing to meet her gaze. "Aleister, what's wrong?"

The Sky Fox stared out the cockpit window. "No. The *Kruetzet* belongs to you... Kalla Melaricsdottr." Shock flooded his mind. Behind him he heard Kalla sink into the gunner's chair with a shaky sob.

"How... how... you... Are you saying the Argosian you took up with was my father...?"

"Melaric Wolffsson, yes." Aleister turn to face her, slipping a small, leather wrapped package from one of his pouches. "This also rightly belongs to you."

Kalla took the package from him and gently unwrapped it. Within was a photograph of her father and her when they were much younger. Kalla remembered when the picture had been taken. Ventaal had been the one to take it. Tears welled up in her eyes and she angrily tried to fight them away as she shook out the other object in the pouch. It was a ring on a thick gold chain; the ring worn by Argosian captains, a gold band set with a brilliant ruby that was engraved with the Trinity Claw of the Argosian Empire.

It was the sight of the ring that opened the floodgates. All of the pent up emotions surrounding her father's death came crashing back and she lost the battle with her tears. Kalla clutched the ring, her father's ring, in her hand and cried all the tears she had kept inside all these many years. Aleister knelt beside the chair, putting his arm around her, murmuring softly.

She buried her face against his shoulder, grieving until the tears came no longer and she finally felt that she had properly sent her father's spirit on. The mage didn't move, but spoke to the magister from where her head was buried against his shoulder.

"How. How did you put those pieces together?" she murmured. Aleister gently drew away from her, standing as he did.

"I... Inari showed me many images. Most I have no idea what they were to mean. He said I would understand in time. He also showed me scenes from your life and from mine. So you see, the ship is yours by right," he said softly. The mage was silent for a moment.

"Thank you. Thank you for sharing this with me." She wrapped the ring and picture back up, tucking them in a hidden pocket. "However, I know he'd want you to have the ship. The *Stymphalian* will remain in your very capable hands."

"You are not angry, milady?"

"No, why should I be?" she asked, puzzlement filtering through the bond. He sighed with relief.

"I don't know. I figured you might be, especially after you got so upset at my being *kitsune*."

"I am angry over neither," she replied.

"I know that now. You don't feel angry. You did at first, but not today. I just wish to make sure." His lilting voice gained confidence now that the situation had been weathered and the mage realized just how worried he'd been over her reaction. She reached out and gave his hand a comforting squeeze.

"You're not getting rid of me that easy. We're in this together. No regrets. Over any of it," she laughed. Aleister returned the squeeze.

"No regrets."

Cryshal Kanlon

Stymphalian, 10000ft above Evalyce, Year of the Golden Hart, 2013 CE

Kalla glared out the window, brooding and silent. As they fast approached Cryshal, she grew more and more anxious. The mage chafed at the thought of being confined to the Kanlon until their 'training' was complete, not after what they had learned. She wanted to be out doing something.

It was late afternoon when they first came in sight of Cryshal Kanlon. The home of the magi was a skycity, like Sevfahl. Ships known as striders patrolled the Kanlon's airspace. They allowed the ship and wyvern to pass unmolested. Kalla grinned to herself when she heard Aleister's low whistle. Even from this far away it was hard to miss the Kanlon. The four House Spires soared upward, flanking the Great Spire as all reached to embrace the sky. The entire facility was cut from a single massive chunk of dark royal amethyst that glittered in the late afternoon sun. On a bright, sunny day the Kanlon could blind pilots with its brilliance if they weren't careful. The windows of the striders were tinted dark for protection.

Not even the magi themselves were sure of how Cryshal had been created. Its existence predated even the oldest records in the Vaults. Kalla had to admit, the Kanlon was one of the most gorgeous and awe-inspiring sights she'd ever seen. All around Cryshal spread the city that supported it- Port Cryshal.

As the *Stymphalian* overflew the farmlands of Port Cryshal, the radio crackled to life.

"*Argosian airship, make landing at the paddocks at Bensen'gar. The wyvern has permission to hunt within the Bensen'gar game forest. She is remain confined there.*" Kalla made a face at the self-importance in the man's voice as she picked up the radio. From her magister she felt a wave of irritation.

"Acknowledged. We will make for Bensen'gar." The voice didn't deign to respond, so Kalla shrugged and clipped the radio back in place. She pointed Aleister in the right direction to reach the Bensen'gar airship paddocks. The magister brought the ship to ground and, following the direction of the flagmen, snugged the ship into a long-term hanger. He sighed as he powered the ship down. That they had been directed to the long-term hanger meant that they wouldn't be flying anytime soon. Kalla exited the ship and waited while Aleister set the security system. As an added protection, she wrapped the ship in several spells to keep people from either snooping or tampering with it. Amaterasu was waiting at the far end of the paddocks. When she saw them, she ignored the flagmen and gave several fluttering hops that brought her to them.

"Amaterasu, they want you to keep to the Bensen'gar forest while we are here. You have free rein of the forest, but you must not leave it," Kalla said.

I understand, Lady Mage. I will go to the forest and wait until you finish your learning. You will come visit?

"Yes, Amaterasu, we will come visit." Kalla patted the wyvern's snout affectionately and pointed the way to Bensen'gar. Amaterasu took off in a flurry of wings as a pair of men dressed in the livery of the Kanlon approached the pair. They bowed and Kalla nodded acknowledgment.

"Lady kyl'Solidor, Magister, if you will please follow us, we have transport waiting for you," one said.

A carriage pulled by Rang'moori horses stood just outside the paddock gates. One of the men held the door open and waited patiently as mage and magister climbed inside, then shut the door behind them. The men climbed atop the carriage and Kalla heard one click his tongue to start the horses moving.

Kalla and Aleister stared out the windows at the passing scenery, as fields and forest flew by. Quaint houses dotted the landscape. They dozed, only to be woken by the staccato sound of hooves striking stone and Kalla glanced out the window. Port Cryshal swept around them, engulfing them in a riot of sounds and smells. People scurried out of the way of the Kanlon carriage. Beyond, the Kanlon itself loomed on the horizon.

They reached the gates and clattered into the main courtyard. Kalla politely thanked the servants who held the doors for them. She turned her gaze to the place that had been home for a great portion of her life. Up close the Kanlon was even more awe-inspiring. Night had come and its eerie shape rose above them, towering over their heads like a giant spiky flower.

Cryshal Kanlon, 10000ft above Evalyce, Year of the Golden Hart, 2013 CE

A mage was there to greet them when they entered the Kanlon proper. He was slightly overweight, with the blond hair and blue eyes common to the Rang'moori. He leaned against an ironwood staff with an *ostrylim* bear climbing the top. Tiny chips of zarconite set for eyes glittered in the light. Kalla dipped a low bow, fist to heart. She shivered slightly, wondering where this man's magister was hiding. A former Ishkaran Nightingale, the man could hide in plain sight and he unnerved Kalla more than even Shingar did.

A dry chuckle brought her attention to Vander, standing hidden until now behind Grosso tem'Solidor. As impossible as it seemed, the flame-haired mage looked even more gaunt than he had the last time she'd seen him. Vander had always been on the thin side, but now he looked ill. His angular face had a drawn, haggard cast to it. The Dashmari's ears were pricked forward and his mane of hair was fluffed in an aggressive manner. Kalla frowned as she noticed that one of his ears looked like it had been shredded and inexpertly healed. The War Mage carried no staff, but here within the Kanlon that wasn't as uncommon.

It was said that the Dashmari were descended from the wolf god, Kituk. She didn't know much about them, save for they were a fierce people whose society was patterned after the great frost wolves. All Dashmari had wolf-like ears, but Vander was a rarity among his people with his flame-colored hair. He strode forward, sharing a look with Grosso as he passed. For just a brief moment he seemed to hunch in on himself, ears relaxing, head held at an odd angle as if he didn't want to meet the Tem's gaze. Grosso scowled at him.

"Well, now. Our errant 'wolf' has returned home." Vander turned a malevolent, icy gaze to Aleister. "And with a magister in tow. It's about time. Can't have you running around like you're better than the rest of us, now can we?"

Kalla ground her teeth together and refused to rise to the bait. If they had chosen the arrogant Dashmari to be her trainer she was going to be very unhappy.

"You *are* her magister, aren't you?" the War Mage growled. Aleister tensed, his shared irritation growing.

"I am, milord," he replied in a polite but stilted voice.

Vander snickered. "Right proper, aren't you? Where are your weapons?"

Aleister willed a slender pair of Arkaddian blades into existence.

"Magick blades. Very nice. Very nice indeed. Well, then. I see no reason not to begin this training. By your leave, tem'Solidor?" Vander turned a questioning look to the Tem'.

Kalla frowned again as she detected the faintest shadow of fear in the Dashmari's eyes. Grosso merely nodded. He hadn't yet deigned to speak. Just watched them with a cold, impassive gaze. Kalla couldn't take it.

"With due respect, tem'Solidor, I don't think Vander a suitable candidate for my training. We do not work well together," she said.

Grosso turned his impassive gaze on her, a look that brooked no argument.

"You will learn that too, then. Vander is your instructor in this matter," the Master replied in a flat voice. Kalla swallowed her frustration.

"Yes, Master tem'Solidor."

"Just so. Follow me then." Vander led the way to a training courtyard within the depths of the Kanlon. Within waited Shingar, dressed in his spiky black armor. Vander gave him a nod and strode off to the side, gesturing for Kalla to join him.

"First things first. We are going to evaluate your magister's initial skill in a mock battle with Shingar here," the thin Mage said. Alarm flooded her mind, followed by grim determination and, chasing after, the strange unidentifiable emotion. Kalla moved over to Aleister as he nervously eyed Shingar and his war mace. He willed a fox-shaped helm to protect his head.

"I want it noted that I object to this," Kalla said. For a fleeting moment, the Dashmari's ears wilted and he made the same odd gesture towards her, though it seemed to Kalla a bit more exaggerated. Then it passed and he scowled at her. She ignored him and turned her attention to Aleister.

"I'm going to weave a protective shield around you. These shields are always used in training so that people do not get hurt. The training shields are also designed to freeze you if you are struck a mortal blow." She concentrated a moment, weaving the shield around her magister. "Just be careful and do your best. This is only an assessment." The mage gave him a friendly slap on the shoulder and gestured for him to square off against Shingar. She heard him swallow hard as he contemplated the massive man covered in black spikes and leaned closer, whispering in his ear. "He looks like a sea urchin, doesn't he?"

Aleister barked a laugh and went to face his opponent. Kalla stiffened as she realized they were attracting attention. Passersby stopped to watch. Vander explained the rules, then stepped out from the center, standing opposite to Kalla.

At Vander's command, Shingar bellowed and charged forward like an angry bull, swinging his mace in a fierce overhead strike. Aleister darted out of the way, his lack of armor making it easier to move. He ducked and spun, hoping to trip the other magister. He only succeeded in making him more angry and the mace came swinging down at his head again. He rolled away and sprang back up, parrying the next blow with the swords. The Sky Fox found himself at a loss. It had been a long time since he'd done this kind of training and never against someone armored. The skills of an Arkaddian vykr warrior were next to useless here. Back and forth the magisters went for several minutes more before Aleister found his energy starting to flag. He'd done a great job of avoiding the flailing mace, but not been able to use his own weapons any. He stumbled and Shingar pounced, faster than he had any right to be, sending the mace crashing into the Sky Fox's head. The next thing Aleister knew he was on his back, with a crushing, cruel headache. His vision was fuzzy and it sounded like people were speaking in tin cans. He heard Kalla screaming, vaguely felt her anger.

"What the hells happened? Get away from him!" Kalla roared with rage. She sent a wave of air slamming into Shingar, knocking him away from Aleister. Her magister didn't look good. Half his skull looked to be crushed. She used magick to gently tug off the fox-head helm only to find her worst fears confirmed. She whirled around.

"Go get Hauss. NOW! Go get Hauss!" she yelled at the gathered crowd. Several took off running. Kalla turned her attention back to Aleister. She had to get him stabilized. Speaking softly, she urged him to stay awake. He mumbled something incoherent as she gently set her power to work. As she worked she talked to him, trying to keep him awake. So intent was she that Kalla didn't even noticed Hauss was there until the gruff Chief Healer chided her out of the way.

"Enough, child. Leave me tend the wound. Keep his heart and his lungs steady," Hauss said. The magister groaned and tried to pull away from Hauss' rougher treatment. Kalla started talking again, and Aleister focused one glazed, brown eye on her. The other had a shot pupil and didn't track with its mate.

"Kalla..." His voice was weak, barely audible. "Kalla... here, take this. I...want you to have it." He pressed a small glass orb into her hand. "Thank you, milady... for this brief reprieve."

Tears flooded her eyes. "No, Aleister. No. You're going to make it. Hauss is the best. He'll fix you right up, you'll see," Kalla said in a choked voice.

"I... think... not... Please... keep the orb safe. After the light dies, keep it safe," he whispered. She looked down at the orb he'd pushed into her hand. Sure enough, it glowed with a multi-hued light that was fast dimming. As she watched, the orb settled on two colors. Green shot with rose. She clutched it tightly in her hand, continuing to murmur softly to the now silent Sky Fox. For an interminable time they knelt there, she keeping her magister's breathing and heartrate even, Hauss working to heal the nuances of the complicated head wound.

Kalla wasn't aware of the crowd surrounding them. Nor was she aware of exactly when Sevrus sin'Wyvaldor and Malik sin'Solidor had arrived. She only dimly registered the commotion behind her as they tried to ascertain exactly what had happened. One thing did sink in and for it she was grateful. If Aleister survived, they were to be turned over to Warryn kyl'Wyvaldor for training. She spared a small smile, despite her worry. Warryn was her oldest friend. He and Shelk would be far easier to work with. At long last she sensed that Aleister's body was stabilizing on its own.

Hauss sat back, motioning for someone off to the side. Four healers in training came forward, with a sling litter. They gently transferred the magister to the litter and carefully carried him to the Healer's Hall. Kalla trailed along behind, still lost in worry. Some called out to her, trying to get her to stop, but she ignored them and followed Hauss.

While she walked she turned the glass orb over in her hands. Unless she was much mistaken, this would be Aleister's fox-ball. She was touched that he had entrusted it to her. The light had brightened somewhat, which meant that he wasn't dying at least. She froze, staring at the colors swirling within, and the import of what part of his essence lay within the gently pulsing orb.

A soft knock on the door woke Kalla. She groaned softly as she straightened. The mage had spent the entire night keeping vigil by her magister's bed. Healers had been in and out all night, checking to make sure that he remained stable. So far, so good, but head wounds were chancy even *if* mage-treated. There was still a very good chance he wouldn't wake or, if he did wake, that his personality wouldn't be the same.

The knock came again, more insistent this time. Before she could say anything, the door swung open and Hauss strode in. Behind him, a guilty looking Warryn lingered in the doorway. The elderly mage chased Warryn away, telling him to return again in thirty minutes or so. Hauss turned to regard her.

The Chief Healer of Cryshal Kanlon was an older and almost constantly grumpy Arkaddian. His hair was no longer reddish-brown, but a mane of cinnamon-tinged silver pulled up in a traditional Arkaddian bob. When it was down, it cascaded past his shoulders in a shimmering silvery waterfall. Hauss had a broad shouldered frame and Kalla knew that many of the women of the Kanlon found him handsome, despite his age. For herself, she couldn't consider him as anything other than a grandfatherly figure. He had been her mentor when she was going through the grueling training to be maester. Despite his gruff attitude the Healer had a heart of gold. She watched as he carefully examined her magister, noting every twitch and frown he made.

"How's he doing, Master Hauss?"

"Everything looks to be in order." His face softened. "Give it time, child. Give it time. All we can do is wait and see what happens. The others will be in later, to begin the work needed to keep him fit until he recovers."

She nodded. She'd done her fair share of therapy on such patients when she'd worked with the Chief Healer. A yawn brought that critical, penetrating gaze to her.

"Go get some food and rest yourself, Kalla. You know better. He'll be fine in our care." Hauss' look told her he'd forcibly carry out his orders if he needed to. She knew he would too. Hauss never made idle threats. He made promises.

Kalla rose from the chair. "Do they know what happened yet? There was nothing wrong with my shield. I've made them numerous times," she said.

"Indeed. There was nothing wrong with your shield, child. Shingar's weapon was enchanted to break through it, though they still aren't sure how." The Healer sighed unhappily. "Master Sevrus has locked both Vander and Shingar in the Great Spire. Vander's power has been bound. He is no threat to you any longer. You should know, though, that Grosso is fighting against his exile, fighting against even a permanent binding," Hauss replied. Kalla ran her hands through her hair.

"No, it does not surprise me... With all respect, Grosso should never have paired me with the War Mage in the first place."

"I know, child. Go now. Get some sleep," Hauss said gently. Kalla nodded and with a last glance back at Aleister's still form, she turned and left.

Warryn greeted her further down the hallway and accompanied her to the dining hall. The Rang'Moori mage was the assistant to the Chief Archivist. Warryn ran a hand through his curly blond hair as he hurried to keep up with Kalla.

"I'm sorry, Kalla. I'm so sorry to hear about what happened."

The mage shook her head, not trusting herself to speak. She fought a losing battle to keep control of her emotions. A thin whimper escaped her and then she was leaning against the wall, sobs shaking her small frame.

"Why, Warryn. Why would they have tried to kill him? What had he ever done to them. He'd never even met them."

The next thing she knew, someone had swept her off her feet. Through her tears she registered that it was Shelk, Warryn's magister. The big Copper Islander held her easily.

"I don't know, Kalla. I can't answer that. Let's get you to your rooms. We can have food brought up for you."

Kalla didn't try to fight Shelk. In her current state, it would have been a losing battle. Warryn's blue eyes were full of concern. As they walked he kept up a stream of mindless banter, asking Kalla questions about her travels. She mumbled replies, trying her best not to lose control again. They reached her rooms in Spire Solidor in a matter of minutes. Apparently the servants had already aired them. There was even a fire going in the fireplace. Shelk carefully set her down on the bed and she wiped a hand across her face.

"Thank you, Shelk. I'm sorry you had to carry me."

"It was no problem, Lady Kalla. I will go and have them bring you something to eat." Shelk's molasses voice rolled over her, bringing with it a measure of calm. His broad, dark face broke into a grin.

"Do not worry about the Arkaddian, Lady Mage. He will be fine. You would not choose one who was weak. He will get better and then we will teach you properly," Shelk rumbled. Kalla returned a shaky smile.

"I hope so," she said. He nodded and strode out of the room in search of a servant, ignoring the bell-pull in order to give Kalla time to compose herself. She turned her attention back to Warryn. "I'm very glad that the Sin' assigned you and Shelk to train us, after..." Her voice trailed off. Warryn grinned.

"I look forward to it." His grin faded as Kalla's face crumpled again. He sat down beside her, wrapping an arm around her and hugging her close.

"I'm sorry, Warryn. I don't know what's gotten in to me." Without thinking, she pulled the fox-ball out of her pocket, rolling it around in her hand. Its light still shone steady, though not brightly.

"It's understandable, Kalla. It's not a crime to care and the two of you *are* bound to one another." He peered closer. "Is that what I think it is? Where'd you get it?" She clutched the orb protectively, even though he hadn't made a move to take it. "Easy, there. I'm not going to snatch it from you," he said gently. She laughed softly.

"Sorry. And yes, it is a *kitsune* orb. It belongs to Aleister."

"Where'd he get it?" Warryn asked.

"No, it *is* his." Kalla went on to explain their adventures on Argoth. Warryn whistled softly.

"So your magister is one of the fox-kin, huh." He tapped the orb. "You realize what he gave you, right?" he asked. She smiled sadly.

"I know. I don't know why, but I know," she replied in a muted voice. Warryn started to say something else, but his words were cut off by the returning Shelk. The big magister carried a tray with a plate of potato dumplings and a flask of fury wine. He put the tray on the table near the door and handed a small packet to Warryn.

"Master Hauss said to make sure she took this," the big Copper Islander said. Kalla scowled at Warryn and Shelk, but didn't object as Warryn mixed the powder with the wine.

"Well now, you should get a nice long sleep in." The pair stayed with her until she finally drifted off into sleep, then quietly snuck out with the tray.

By the time the mage woke again, it was dark. She'd slept the entire day. Kalla unconsciously cast her mind in search of Aleister only to be forcibly reminded that he was in a coma. After all these weeks of contact, the lack of thoughts brought a wash of loneliness over her. She pulled out the orb. It still shone faintly, green and rose swirling around one another. Pocketing it, she made her way back to the Healer's Hall. As she arrived at his room, two healers were leaving. They gave her a thumbs up sign that she took to mean that he was still stable. Not that she didn't trust them, but she did her own evaluation. Sure enough, all was well. She just needed to be patient. Too bad patience was something those of House Solidor tended to lack.

For that night and every one after she continued to keep her vigil. Days turned to weeks. She often helped with her magister's therapy and got to know all of the trainees quite well. Hauss had a promising bunch this time, especially in Manny Malkador. The young healer was one of the Plains people, but from Sveldtland rather than Arkaddia. Sveldtlanders had the same coffee-colored skin, but tended towards black hair rather than reddish-brown. He was almost always a part of the therapy team working with Aleister. Several more times Hauss had Warryn haul her away and dose her to make her sleep. A few times she had ridden out to Bensen'gar to visit Amaterasu. The wyvern was saddened to hear about Aleister and delighted to meet Warryn and Shelk.

Twice Kalla spoke before the Sin' and Tem' regarding her claims that Al'dhumarna was stirring. Of them all, Grosso still stood against her. Thankfully the Sin' took her more seriously. Master Sevrus assured her they were looking into it. Numerous reports of bizarre happenings came in daily now. Floods in the Plainslands were ruining the lush grass seas. Drought in Rang'Moori was creating a desert that spread at an alarmingly unnatural rate. Groundcities were still susceptible to attack. Even the skycities still found themselves approached by smaller bands of wyvern, but they were more vigilant now and well-protected by anti-airship guns.

Vander had been allowed to stay in the Kanlon. His powers were still bound and he and Shingar were still guests of the Great Spire. Part of her would have liked to have confronted him, demanded answers; part of her was scared what might happen if she did. Winter settled around Cryshal Kanlon, muting its glow and blanketing the surrounding fields. The Solstice Celebration fast approached, but Kalla's heart wasn't in it.

* * *

Aleister groaned and cracked one eye open. He found himself in a dimly lit room. In the waning light outside he could see that it was snowing. Why was it snowing? It had been fall when they'd gotten here. The Magister frowned. That was the last thing he remembered, landing at the Bensen'gar paddocks. He sought out Kalla's mind, but found her asleep. He closed his eyes again, listening to voices in the hall. With a small scraping sound, the door to his room opened and an older Arkaddian man stepped into the room. When he saw that Aleister was awake the scowl left his face and he smiled. He turned to the person behind them, instructing them to go fetch Kalla.

"Well now, son. I was afraid you were never going to wake up. I'd almost given up hope on you."

"Given up hope?" Aleister frowned at the hoarseness of his voice. The Arkaddian came closer and rested his hands against the Sky Fox's temples. Aleister drew back at the touch.

"Easy, son. I just want to see how things are looking. You took a pretty bad blow to the head." He stepped back, satisfied with what he found. Aleister ran a hand over the area. A small depression was all that remained as a mute testament to the wound that had felled him. "My name's Hauss. I'm the Chief Healer here." Hauss took a seat on the wooden chair beside the bed. "Son, you've been in a coma for six weeks. If you hadn't been here, of all places, you wouldn't have survived."

Aleister shook his head. "The last thing I remember is arriving at Bensen'gar." He blinked as a flood of emotion engulfed him. A soft crack of power and his mage stood before them. Hauss scowled, but it softened as Kalla knelt beside the bed.

"You're awake. Great Balgeras, you're awake." Something shimmered on her cheeks in the dim light. The Fox reached out and carefully wiped away a tear.

"You... you would weep for me?" he asked softly. Kalla gave a shaky laugh, but said nothing. She merely took his hand and squeezed it gently. A soft knock on the door and Manny came through, carrying a mug of something that steamed gently. As Kalla helped Aleister to sit up, Manny handed the mug to Hauss and departed. Hauss passed the mug to Aleister.

"Drink up, son. This will help you sleep more naturally and to build your strength. I'm going to ask you a few questions, just to see what might be affected." Aleister nodded as he gingerly took a sip from the steaming mug. It didn't taste as bad as he'd been afraid it might. Between the two Healers they asked a great many questions and he felt Kalla's relief grow as he apparently answered each to their satisfaction. Sometimes the instructions were to move a hand or a foot. Sometimes it was nonsensical things like naming animals alphabetically. Finally, even Hauss was satisfied that all was in order. By now Aleister was pleasantly relaxed and wanted nothing more than to snug down in the blankets and go back to sleep. Hauss departed, but not before admonishing Kalla to return to her quarters and get some rest herself. After the Chief Healer left, she turned back to Aleister.

"Here, this belongs to you." She held out the fox-ball, now shining brightly. He stared at it for a moment, then his eyes flicked up to look at her. He looked away, out the now dark window.

"No, you keep it. It was freely given."

"Aleister, do you understand what you have done in giving me this?"

"Yes. . . " His voice trailed off. Through the re-established bond she felt his exhaustion and the hurt she had caused by trying to return the orb. Beneath those ran the odd undercurrent she kept sensing, but couldn't grasp. Even now, he was pushing them down. She tucked the orb away and knelt beside the bed as he shrugged himself back down so he could sleep. Even that was enough to double his exhaustion.

"I'm sorry, Aleister. I just wanted to be sure." She reached out and brushed his hair back. The hurt feeling diminished as he leaned against the touch. He murmured something she couldn't understand, something in Arkaddian, before drifting off into a more natural sleep. Now that the bond was back, Kalla realized how much she'd missed it. Even when he was asleep, it was a comforting presence in the back of her mind. After she was sure he was asleep, Kalla crept from the room. She made her way back to her own rooms where she promptly downed the rest of the fury wine potion Warryn had left with her and offered a prayer of thanks to Balgeras.

Aleister felt much better in the morning. He wolfed down the breakfast Hauss brought him, answering yet another series of questions while he did so. Hauss sat down in the wooden chair beside the bed again, casting his eyes up to the ceiling.

"Warryn and Rosalia are going to keep Kalla away for awhile. We need to have a talk, son," Hauss said. Aleister gave the Healer a puzzled look.

"I know who you are, son. I know what you've done," Hauss rumbled. The Sky Fox blanched at these words.

"How…"

"Easy, son. I understand why you did it. I saw your memories while I was healing you. You might be happy to know you still have family living," the Healer said, his gruff voice gentle. Aleister rubbed a hand over his face.

"Family? Where?"

"You're looking at him, son." Hauss tapped the Magister on the forehead. "I'd be your uncle, if I were still in Arkaddia."

"If you were still in Arkaddia you would be obligated to kill me," Aleister replied.

"Aye, glad I am that I'm not, then. I like you, son." He paused for a moment, favoring Aleister with a penetrating gaze. "Tell me, do you understand the Fox King's visions?" Hauss asked. Aleister gave the Chief Healer a hard look before turning to look out the window. Snow piled against it now, but the day beyond was clear and bright.

"I understand those about my past. I understand that Kalla was Melaric's daughter. The rest, no I'm afraid not," he said softly. Hauss snorted.

"They were all you. And Kalla. She was right, boy. Your first incarnation in this world was *kitsune*. And hers? She was the frost wolf. She was the hunter. She was the captain to your gunner. She was the Kymry healer to your sheepherder. She was one of the Arkaddian generals, you were the other. She was the merchant's wife, you were the merchant." Hauss cast another glance upwards. Through the bond, Aleister felt Kalla's growing irritation.

"Shards! She won't be deterred much longer. Son, my point is, the pair of you have been drawn together life after life. No

95

doubt a strong bond was formed in your first encounter. I can't say. I would bet, though, that she was unconsciously drawn to you during her search for a magister and thus the pair of you find yourselves together again."

"I-"

"I know, son, you're Arkaddian, you don't believe in past lives. They don't require your belief. I can also tell you that you need to tell her about your past." With this last, the Healer turned and opened the door, revealing an irritated Kalla. The mage stalked into the room, muttering darkly.

"Why does everyone and their brother feel the need to ask my opinion on something this morning..." she growled.

"I have no idea, Kalla. However, you'll be happy to know that we can get your magister up and moving about today. It'll be a few more days before he'll be ready to leave the Healer's Hall, but he's still doing nicely. They did well with his therapy."

"I'm right here, remember," Aleister said. Hauss jumped with a mock look of surprise. He gave Aleister a friendly slap on the leg as he left.

"Remember what I said, son." Kalla gave the Healer's departing back another odd look.

"Remember what?" she asked.

"It's nothing. Just some tips on getting better." Kalla's look said she didn't believe him, but before she could question him further, Manny and another of the healers came in.

"Feel up to a bath?"

Aleister nodded and the pair helped him to stand. Though his legs were shaky at first, he gained a bit of strength as he walked. Kalla watched them lead him down the hall and then set off in search of Warryn. By the time lunch rolled around she could tell he'd worn himself out and Hauss had dosed him with the sleeping draught again. Over the next several days the Sky Fox showed vast improvements. Hauss finally released him from the Healer's Hall with the warning to be careful and to return each

Endday for an evaluation. In short order he soon found himself in quarters within House Solidor, nearer to his mage.

Wolf in the Fold

Cryshal Kanlon, 10000ft above Evalyce, Year of the Golden Hart, 2013 CE

Kalla and Aleister joined Warryn and Shelk out in the Solidor courtyard. The House courtyards were kept shielded from the winter weather. Inside they were warm, dry and free of the snow that still covered the grounds. Mage and magister were finally going to begin the training they had come here for in the first place.

"Rule number one, always have fun!" The Rang'Moori mage grinned at them. "Remember to enjoy life. It's too short as it is." He grew more serious. "Aleister, I'd like you to go with Shelk. He will be taking care of your physical training. Return here in an hour." As the two magisters departed, Warryn turned his attention back to Kalla. "Now for your part- latch onto his thoughts. Follow them. See if you can trace their path in your mind," he murmured. Kalla nodded and closed her eyes. For several long moments she was silent.

"I think… they are in the Malkador courtyard. That seems about right," she said.

"Correct! Now, picture the scene in your mind. You are there with them. What do you see?" For the next hour Warryn had her describing every little detail of what she thought she saw. The skills themselves were ones magi learned early on. The trick lay in processing them through their magisters' minds. From Shelk Warryn confirmed when Kalla got something right. After an hour, the magisters returned and knelt in the grass beside the magi.

"Not too bad for a first session. Now we are going to work on strengthening the bond between you. By the time we are done with the training, you should be able to actively influence the bond and to communicate telepathically with one another. You will need to learn to buff your mental shields to keep stray thoughts from wandering."

Aleister paled at this last. Kalla gave him a look of concern, but didn't say anything.

"Now then, I want both of you to actively concentrate on the bond between you," Warryn said.

For the next two hours the Archivist had the two of them doing all kinds of mental exercises. He finally called a halt and both mage and magister slumped in relief.

"I thought I had passed all of this learning stuff long ago. You could almost put Hauss to shame, Warryn!" Kalla exclaimed. The Archivist aimed a swat at her but she ducked out of the way.

"We'll meet here tomorrow at the same time," he said. The four left, heading to the dining hall where dinner was just being served.

For the next two weeks they followed the same pattern. Aleister would begin his days with Shelk and Kalla had to follow him in her mind. When the magisters returned, she and Aleister had to tackle the grueling mental tasks Warryn set for them. It was Fenrix of their second week when they had a major breakthrough.

"*Aleister!*" Kalla's voice sounded in his mind. The magister spooked but didn't let his guard down. He blocked a swing by the big Copper Islander and backed up, trying to figure out how to respond.

"*Yes?*" His mindvoice was tentative and he wasn't sure he'd actually responded to the mage's mental call.

"*You did it!*" A pause "*Warryn says come back. That's enough for today. We've done well.*" Pride came through the shared link.

"*Yes, milady.*" Even as Kalla was relaying this, Shelk was receiving the same message from Warryn. Aleister had come to recognize the look the big magister got when Warryn was speaking with him. After he'd learned to recognize it in Shelk, he began to see the same look in others he came across and he judged them to be magisters also, even if not in company of a mage. Here in the Kanlon, the guardians were given more freedom to wander. He'd also discovered that not all magisters were male. There were female magisters, most often bonded to males, but not always. Warryn's brother, Warryck, had a female magister as did Hauss.

Aleister still found it hard to believe that the Arkaddian Healer was his uncle. His father had never even mentioned having a brother who had been taken away to the Kanlon. The magisters rejoined their magi in the Solidor courtyard. Once they were all assembled, Warryn cast a critical eye over the pair, before he broke out in a big grin.

"You've done well. Seeing as how tomorrow is the Solstice Celebration, I say we enjoy the next few days. We'll begin again on Balgrix."

"A few days to relax sounds nice." said Kalla.

Warryn grinned. "Now, it's not been that bad!"

The four broke up, going their separate ways for the day. Kalla toyed with the idea of going to see Amaterasu, but decided against it. Though they had ended the session earlier than usual, it would be nearly dark by the time she and Aleister reached Bensen'gar. Besides, they had two free days. They could spend the whole day after Solstice with the wyvern, maybe even taking the airship out. Kalla wandered to the Healer's Hall, Aleister trailing along behind.

Rosalia greeted them at the door. The plump Rang'Moori broke out into a wide grin when they entered, her blue eyes twinkling. Rosalia was an herbalist at the Hall. She also happened to be Hauss's magister and lady wife.

"Come in, come in! Hauss is testing new Healers at the moment. We have a few he thought ready to become maesters. He should be almost done. You'll stay for supper with us?" Rosalia asked. Kalla laughed.

"Oh my. I don't envy those poor people. Who're the lucky ones?"

"Well, the two Aerodor sisters, Leskin Wyvaldor and... Manny Malkador. Yes, that should be all of them," the herbalist replied.

"And I wish the best of luck to them! Yes, Rosalia, if you'll have us for supper, I think we'll stick around. Warryn's finished with us today," Kalla said.

"How is your training going, dear?" asked Rosalia. Kalla grinned again.

"We managed telepathic contact finally. Warryn gave us the next two days off," she said. The elder magister beamed with pride and swept Kalla up in a grandmotherly hug.

"That's wonderful, dears. Hauss will be proud of both of you." Rosalia let go of Kalla and swept the Sky Fox in an equally generous hug. She got a thoughtful look in her eye. "Speaking of which, here he comes." Sure enough Hauss entered the Healer's Hall, followed by the younger Sveldtlander, who was beaming.

"I take it you passed?" Kalla asked. His grin told her all she needed to know. "Well, congratulations then, Manny kyl'Malkador."

"Thanks! Guess I'll be leaving next week to acquire my own magister. I only hope I'm as lucky as the two of you. I'd like to find someone with whom I can work as well with as you and Hauss work with Aleister and Rosalia," Manny said.

"I'm sure you will, son. Congratulations on a job well done. You've exceeded my expectations," said Hauss. Here Kalla laughed.

"Then I *know* you did well. Hauss sets high expectations of all his students," Kalla said. The elder Arkaddian scowled at her. "Well, you do. You can't deny it." She laughed again and Hauss relented with a sly grin of his own.

"No, but look how well both of you turned out," Hauss said. He turned back to Manny. "Any other questions, son?"

"No... well. Yeah, one, I guess. Why, exactly, do we seek out magisters from criminals?" Manny asked.

Kalla snorted. Hauss gestured for her to answer and Aleister perked up. It was a question he had often wondered, but hadn't dared to ask. He didn't want to seem ungrateful for the second chance he'd been given.

"Magisters are chosen from the ranks of the walking dead, ostensibly because it was assumed that those convicted of such crimes warranting death would be strong enough to both serve as fierce protection for a recuperating Mage and as a stalwart source of extra power if needed. The bond is designed to ensure that the recipient does not accept to merely gain freedom, then slay the mage to escape. If a mage dies, then so will their magister. However, the reverse is not true, though you will feel the death." Her voice grew softer, "... and you will feel it if the bond is broken for some other reason, such as a coma. An emptiness where you are used to sensing something. It is not... pleasant. At any rate, as you can see, many of us have found ways to circumvent having an unpleasant companion. I don't regret my choice, though I do regret having had to do it in the first place. It is a form of enslavement and that does not sit well with me."

"I see. It still doesn't make much sense to me, especially if you have someone willing to take the bond," Manny said with a frown.

"Well, Warryn knows the history and lore better than I do, but the reasoning there was because you ran the risk of magi limiting their power for fear of hurting their magisters, or killing them when they themselves died. Sometimes it comes down to the good of the many versus the good of the one. A mage might be willing to risk their own life if need be, but not that of the one bonded to them. The mage and magister become good friends, or even husband and wife."

Manny nodded. "I think I understand a bit better now. Thank you, Lady-"

"You are a maester in your own right, Lord kyl'Malkador," Kalla chided. "Call me Kalla."

The Sveltlander shook his head. "That's going to take some getting used to."

"Before you know it, it'll seem natural. You wish to stay with us for supper?" Hauss asked.

"No thank you, Master Hauss. I think I'd like to eat in my quarters tonight. I have much to think about." Manny made his farewells and the four made their way to the office that Rosalia and Hauss shared. In short order servants had brought up plates of savory potato dumplings, roast duck, brown bread and steaming mugs of spiced fury wine. The meal passed in meaningless banter as the fury wine slowly relaxed them. It hadn't taken long for Aleister to realize that magisters did, indeed, acquire the same alcohol tolerance as their magi. As supper ended the conversation turned to Kalla and Aleister's success of the day.

"Shards! That was fast. It usually takes months for most to reach that point." Hauss turned his penetrating gaze on Aleister, all trace of the fury wine's relaxing effect vanishing from his countenance. He gestured towards Kalla. "Tell her, son. Before you share unshielded memories. And it will happen, believe me."

The Sky Fox flinched at the elder Arkaddian's words. His entire body tensed, flooded sudden by battle-readiness, ready to attack or flee. He swallowed hard when Kalla turned to him.

"Tell me what?" she asked. Aleister wilted under her questioning gaze, terrified of what she would think of him after she found out, especially after the reaction to his new form. He lowered his gaze to the table top.

"Take the memories from my mind," he whispered.

"Very well. Give me your hand." Kalla took the proffered hand, puzzled at the shame and fear she was sensing from Aleister. She glanced at Hauss and the mage gave her a curt nod, his face set in harsh lines. Though he really didn't want to put his young nephew through this, now was better than later. Hauss watched as Kalla frowned, then her face went slack as she was pulled into her magister's memories. Her gaze became unfocused, staring at nothing. She remained that way for several moments before letting go of his hand.

Kalla shook her head to clear it, her gaze returning to normal. From Aleister, she still felt shame and fear. She reached out and gave his hand a gentle squeeze.

"It's okay. I already knew. You did what you had to do."

Aleister risked a glance up at her and she smiled. He felt his shame and fear begin to dissipate.

"But... how did you already know?" he asked.

"I saw those memories when I was working to heal you, before Hauss arrived. That's all I saw though. The other memories you shared were new. Were they the visions the Fox King gave you?"

Aleister nodded uncertainly. "Yes, milady. Hauss... helped me to understand some of them. He said they were past lives. But... I still have trouble believing that," he said.

Kalla frowned as the puzzle pieces of new information fell in place.

"If you will excuse me." Kalla's voice was absentminded.

Hauss and Rosalia nodded. Aleister started to follow her, but a motion from Hauss kept him in his chair. He gave a shaky sigh as his mage disappeared.

"Well, that went quite well, son. I figured she might have already known." Hauss clapped him on the shoulder.

Aleister narrowed his eyes at the elder Arkaddian.

"Then why-"

"I also knew you wouldn't speak up. Far better to take care of it now than when you were training. There was always the slight chance she didn't know and finding out that way would not have made her happy," Hauss said. Aleister wilted.

"Guess not..."

"I know 'not', son. She was my student remember. Oh yes, while you're here, we might as well get your check-up for the week done. Close enough to tomorrow anyway."

Aleister shrugged and waited patiently while Hauss evaluated him and put him through the weekly questioning. Satisfied, the Chief Healer let him leave and the Sky Fox wandered to his quarters. Through the link he sensed that Kalla was not quite asleep. Rather, she was in one of the deep trances he had learned to associate with journeying. Aleister rifled through the stack of books he had borrowed from the Kanlon library. Finding one of particular interest- a slim volume of Argosian lore- Aleister settled to read.

* * *

Morning dawned bright and cold, a promising beginning to the Winter Solstice. Sunlight streaming through the window woke Aleister and he groaned, dismayed to find he'd fallen asleep while reading. His neck and shoulders were stiff from sleeping sitting up. He stood and stretched, sending his mind in search of his mage. Wherever she was, her mind was guarded and he couldn't quite place her. He wandered down to the dining hall where he found Warryn and Shelk.

"Where is Kalla, milord? I ... eh... can't sense her," Aleister asked.

Both Warryn and Shelk broke out into big grins.

"No doubt. She is closeted with Hauss, the Sveldtlander Healer and a few others. They are working on something for the feast, something that's to be a surprise to you. She asked that Shelk and I keep you entertained for the day," Warryn replied.

The next few hours passed in a blur, as Aleister learned how to play *chigali* from the Archivist and his magister. The game, popular among the magi, was played on a gridded 10 x 10 game board, and was designed to teach strategic thinking. Each player had twenty pieces. Here at the Kanlon, the pieces were color coded to different Houses. The game was so popular that most magi kept a personal set of pieces with them and were more than happy to play at a moment's notice. As a Solstice gift, Warryn gave Aleister his own set of pieces, Artisan-crafted from deep red garnet.

The Sky Fox took to the game like a fish to water, so easily did cunning strategy come to him. Even so, Warryn gave him more than a run for his money. Aleister was more evenly matched with Shelk, though the quiet magister was content to sit in the sunlight streaming through the library windows and read. Aleister smiled ruefully. Before meeting Kalla and Warryn, he'd never cared too much for reading. Now, he found he quite enjoyed it. The Archivist's love of learning seemed to rub off on those he was close to. They spent hours absorbed in the nuances of the game, and before they knew it the big bell of the Kanlon was ringing out to announce the beginning of the feast.

"Guess we lost track of time," Warryn said with a grin, "C'mon. We should get to the Great Hall."

Aleister followed Warryn and Shelk, casting his mind for Kalla once more. As before, he found his mind blocked. They entered the Great Hall and Aleister gaped at the changes. Whereas before the huge room had been lined with bench after bench in neat, tidy rows, there were now low tables spread out all over the floor. Cushions were piled around them, serving as seats.

However, what drew his attention more than anything were the massive Arkaddian thunder drums set up on the dais at the far end of the room.

Aleister followed Warryn and Shelk to one of the tables nearest the dais, where Rosalia was already saving them a seat. He settled down, still focused on the thunder drums. There was a single great-drum flanked by twin bull-drums. Fanning out from each side of the bull-drums were two side-drums and two ground-drums. Several drummers walked onto the stage, led by a tall Arkaddian whose long silver hair was pulled back into a loose tail.

The man wore baggy pants and was bare-chested save for a sash woven blue and silver across his chest. In his hands he twirled the strikers used to beat the biggest of the drums- a monstrosity that stood two feet taller than the tall Arkaddian. Aleister blinked as he realized the man was Hauss. As he studied them he recognized several of the other drummers as well, all Healers. The drummer bearing the twins to Hauss' strikers was the Sveltlander Healer, Manny. His jaw dropped when another of the drummers came close and he realized it was Kalla. His mage wore baggy pants similar to Hauss' and an equally loose-fitting tunic. Kalla's hair was pulled back into a bob and she carried a set of smaller strikers. She took a place at one of the side-drums closest to where the Sky Fox sat with Warryn and Shelk. Waving to them, she released the block that had kept him from finding her all day. Her mind bubbled with laughter at his thoughts.

"*Surprised?*" she asked.

"*Just a little...*" Aleister replied.

The rest of the drummers took their places at the side-drums, bull-drums, and ground-drums as Hauss and Manny took up their positions at the great-drum. Four more filtered on-stage, bearing shoulder-drums, followed by a mage Aleister didn't recognize. An older Argosian with grey streaking his black hair, his black robes were trimmed in alternating slashes of ruby red, sapphire blue, emerald green, and amber yellow, as all of the 'Sin's robes were. Around his neck he wore a pendant that consisted of the four House Guardians woven around and through the Spiral of Cryshal. Aleister leaned closer to Warryn.

"Who's that? I haven't seen him yet," he asked softly.

"That would be Jasper sin'Solidor, the Grand Maester of the Kanlon. He's the one in charge of everything," Warryn whispered back. Aleister listened as the Grand Maester welcomed them all to the feast. He led them in a brief prayer and toast, before turning the show over to Hauss. The Chief Healer bowed, touching fist to heart.

"I thank you, Master sin'Solidor." He turned to address the crowd. "Well, let's get the show started!"

The crowd roared its approval and the Magister guessed that the thunder drummers were well-beloved acts at Kanlon festivals. As the first notes were struck, he recognized the piece they were playing. It was 'Season of the Blue Wolf', a piece oft played at winter festivals throughout the Arkaddian Empire. His gaze swept the drummers, coming to rest on Kalla. Her eyes were half closed, and she had fallen into a relaxed rhythm with the strikers, easily keeping pace. Her body rocked slightly to the beat of the drums. Aleister was surprised. Mastering any of the thunder drums was difficult, but she played with an ease that belayed long years of practice.

All of the drummers were having the time of their lives. Those with the shoulder-drums danced as they played, weaving in and out among the stationary drums. Aleister watched, mesmerized, until the piece wound to a close some fifteen minutes later, then joined the crowd as they gave the drummers a standing ovation. As one, the thunder drummers bowed to the crowd and filtered off-stage, to be replaced by players bearing pan-pipes and *basacaila,* a stringed instrument unique to the Rang'moori.

Hauss and Kalla joined them then, sinking down onto the soft cushions, both grinning like crazy.

"Where did you learn to play thunder drums, milady?" Aleister asked as they settled down. Kalla laughed.

"Well, Hauss thinks that it provides good discipline. Most of the Healers know how," she replied.

The magister could only shake his head. By this time servants were weaving around the room, placing platters of food on the low tables. Several bustled over to theirs, laying down plates of potato dumplings, roast duck and lamb, baskets of brown bread, salads, trays of fruit and cheese, bowls of rice, and a fish dish that he didn't recognize. Pitchers of fury wine followed, along with a stack of smaller plates. Hauss and Kalla murmured thanks as the servants departed. A few turned and waved at the magi. Aleister followed the example of the others as they each took a smaller plate and filled it. He turned his attention back to the stage, listening to the pan-pipes and *basacaila*. The players finished their piece, to rousing applause. As they drifted off-stage, they were replaced by players bearing Argosian fox-flutes and Dashmari tambourines. As the feast progressed, several more sets were played, alternating between the pan-pipes/ *basacaila* players, and those with the fox-flutes and tambourines.

Soon enough Hauss and Kalla stood up again and made their way back to the stage. Other drummers came up, but not as many as before. This time both Hauss and Kalla took up shoulder-drums, settling them across their backs, before taking places at the great-drum. Aleister frowned. There were few pieces in which one drummer used more than one drum, and all were exceedingly difficult. As Arkaddian and Argosian struck the first notes he realized they had decided to do the hardest of these- the 'Dance of the Dragon'. Aleister snorted a laugh. Why should he be surprised? It seemed that those of House Solidor all tended to push themselves to their limits and beyond, in everything they did.

The pair set up a fast pace, strikers mere blurs as they alternated between striking the great drum and the shoulder drums. As they played, the bull-drums and ground-drums chimed in, creating an intoxicating beat. By the time they had finished, Aleister could tell that Kalla was exhausted. Happy, but exhausted.

The celebration didn't last much longer. It was now late in the night and most were sleepy and content, ready for bed. The magister yawned as he followed Kalla and Hauss. Warryn and Shelk had already bid them goodnight and were heading in the direction of Spire Malkador.

Aleister tensed as he caught an unfamiliar sound, stopping to listen closer. The sound came again, a soft scraping noise. Growling laughter filled the night as a firestorm erupted down the corridor. Aleister jerked Kalla to the ground, even as both magi threw up shields. Hauss, in the lead, took the brunt of the attack, roaring with pain as the flames engulfed him. They tore through his half-formed shields, and the Healer crumpled to the ground. Luckily, Rosalia was closer to Kalla and so had the benefit of the female mage's shields as well.

Kalla jumped up, torn between following their assailant and helping Hauss. She paused long enough to make sure that he was still alive, but more people were flooding the corridor to find out what the commotion was, so she left him in the care of his magister and pounded down the corridor, the Sky Fox right beside her. As he ran, he willed twin Arkaddian swords into existence, along with supple snake-skin armour like that favored by Argoth's Praetorian Guard.

Kalla slowed as she came to the Solidor courtyard. Beyond, there was only gloom and darkness, but she sensed it wasn't as empty as it seemed. The mage carefully strengthened the protective shields and conjured a globe of magelight. She eased into the courtyard, followed by an alert Aleister.

No sooner had both mage and magister entered the courtyard, than a warding swept around it, sealing them in and causing the magelight to wink out. They couldn't leave nor could they expect any help till the warding was broken. The growling laughter came again. With a sound like thunder, the courtyard filled with light, revealing the source. Kalla's jaw dropped. In the center of the courtyard stood Vander and Shingar, the War Mage looking even thinner than the last time she'd seen him. He sent another jet of flame racing towards them, forcing them to jump to either side of the entrance, the fireball barely missing them. It slammed into the ward and dissipated, absorbed into it. Kalla stood carefully, keeping a wary eye on the volatile War Mage.

"*Take care of Shingar. I'll handle the War Mage.*"

"*Yes, milady,*" Aleister growled, moving off to circle around the pair. Vander ignored him, but the spiky magister stepped forward to meet him.

"Think you'll fare any better this time, Fox?" The big magister's voice was deep and gravely, full of contempt.

"I think I've learned from my mistakes," replied Aleister. Shingar snorted, sounding like an angry bull, as the pair engaged in a deadly dance.

Nearby Kalla faced Vander. The Healer wondered how he had freed himself. She approached him warily, noting that his ears were flat and his mane bristled with anger, the long pony-tail draped over his shoulder. For one brief instant his countenance changed. His shoulders slumped, and the ears became submissive rather than angry. The War Mage lifted his head, turning it slightly so that he looked down at her from the corner of his eye.

In the time it took Kall to take a breath, the uncertainty was gone. Lightning crackled in the air, slamming into the ground to all sides of her. Her shields held, but before she could do anything, the War Mage sent another fireball careening into her. She shook her head, casting her own power into the ground. The earth heaved and churned, exploding with a fury, but the War

Mage was by far the more skilled in offensive magick and easily blocked it. Kalla racked her mind for a solution, as more lightning washed over the shields. They wouldn't last much longer under the relentless attack. She was going to have to act fast. Something Hauss had once told her came flooding back to memory.

A Healer is far more dangerous than any other, even the War Magi. Why? Because if a Healer can merely touch a person, he can kill them. Our gift, the nature of it, can surpass even the strongest shield if we can touch the person.

This revelation had been followed by a little demonstration. Hauss had made her shield herself, then reached out and gripped her wrist. The Healer's gift had flooded into her, but instead of healing, he'd frozen her lungs for a second or two. It had been a frightening thought then, to think that her gift could be used in such a way. Unfortunately that way might be the only one now. She needed to goad the War Mage into becoming careless, into getting closer, giving her the chance to touch him. Kalla took a deep breath. Time to take the wolf by the tail. She only hoped her gamble would pay off.

Kalla straightened, recovering from the latest assault. She drew herself to her full height, green eyes blazing. The petite Healer took several steps forward and her bold behavior threw the War Mage off for a moment. He faltered, giving ground. For another instance his shoulders slumped, the ears relaxed, his head turning to the side.

"What's the matter, cubling? You can't tell me you're *afraid* of me," she snarled. The War Mage recoiled and she pressed forward. "That's it isn't it?

"You're weak, Vander kyl'Solidor. You're a disgrace to House Solidor," Kalla hissed out. His reaction was almost instantaneous. The thin Mage snarled back, putting every ounce of strength behind his attack. Lightning twined with fire slammed into her shield. It crumpled like paper and she dropped to the ground, dazed and disoriented. As she struggled to get up, she heard his footsteps come closer. On the far side of the courtyard she could hear Aleister and Shingar. The Sky Fox seemed to be holding his own for the moment.

Vander stopped before her and she looked up at him. The War Mage's face was flushed, and his lips were pulled back, baring his long carnassial teeth. At his sides, his hands were clenched tight. Madness glittered in his icy eyes.

Close enough... Kalla lunged, latching onto his wrist. Vander tried to jerk away, but she'd already sent her power racing through him, freezing his lungs. A look of surprise crossed his face. As he sank to the ground a cold voice slithered through her mind.

Go ahead... end it... this one is of no use to me anymore... Go ahead. Kill him. You know you want to...

Kalla frowned, gazing into Vander's now frightened blue eyes as he slowly suffocated. Yes... she could finish it. There wasn't anything he could do. She could implode his heart, fry his brain, or simply wait until things stopped working on their own, and there wasn't a single thing he could do about it. The cold look on her face was enough to drain the fear from his eyes, replacing it with a look of utter hopelessness. His ears wilted and his eyes fluttered shut, unable to face her empty indifference. He lifted his chin, twisting his head around so that he was almost facing over his shoulder. Kalla finally realized what it meant. It was the gesture of a submissive wolf to one more dominant, baring the throat in an act of silent supplication.

As his life began to fade, images came to the Healer's mind, much as they might when a serious Healing was undertaken. A tiny child, the seventh son in the family, and the only one not born with a twin. Not only that but to be born scrawny and thin and oh so different, with his odd red hair.

A young boy, four years old, beaten half to death for not being strong enough or fast enough. And always the reminder that he 'didn't belong'. The same boy, age nine, with two magi. He had the gift, surely his family would be proud. They weren't. The father was willing to pay to have the 'little freak' taken away.

Scenes flashed by of the boy at the Kanlon, but even there he didn't fit. Small and thin for his age, the fact that he was Dashmari didn't help. The children were cruel as only children could be and the youngster soon learned to keep to himself. Only one other, a young Argosian student, stepped in to stop his torment. The bullies soon learned to fear the one they called 'Wolf that Sleeps' and left him be if she was around, but they made it a point to catch him alone later and then things were twice as bad.

As he grew older, the abuse and his own insecurity bred in him a smoldering rage. The Master of the House noted this and put him through training as a War Mage. It came naturally, but the inherent feeling of weakness was still there and, though he excelled at it, it wasn't what he would have chosen had he been given the choice.

Fast forward a few years and the Dashmari, now grown into a handsome young man, once more approached the Argosian, but was firmly rebuffed. He bottled his hurt and unhappiness into anger, channeling that anger into his studies. Soon enough he was named maester and sent out to find a magister. When he returned with Shingar, the Argosian's dislike was almost palpable. Though a maester already, she had fought tooth and nail against taking a guardian of her own. Years passed and he went and carried out the tasks the Master of Solidor set him. He wasn't sure when, but at some point during his service to Grosso, a voice began to fill his mind. It made promises, if only he would continue to do Grosso's work, for the Master of Solidor served the voice as well.

The lifetime lasted a mere heartbeat before another mind tore through hers in an explosion of power. It wiped away all traces of the insidious voice urging her to kill the War Mage.

Let him go. Let him live.

The voice rasped through her mind, rough as sandpaper. It was the voice of Balgeras, the guardian god of House Solidor. In an electric instant, Balgeras' power jumped to Vander, yet she could still feel it, hear it.

You have a second chance, cubling. Don't mess it up.

Kalla jerked her hand away as Vander's body began shifting. In a moment a man no longer knelt before her, but a great frost wolf lay hunched on the ground, eyes closed. His body heaved as he struggled to draw in breath, flame-colored sides rising and falling. Even in this form, there was a certain gauntness to his frame, though frost wolves were normally stocky, and still he had his long tail of hair, now draped across a back disturbingly laced with uneven scars. One paw scrabbled weakly at the floor, then went still.

He is your responsibility now. My last act. You must tell them-Grosso has broken the tenets. House Solidor has no guardian. The breach must be repaired.

Trust in yourself, Mother of Wolves, believe in yourself. A cheshire grin, unseen. *We shall see you soon enough. Until then...*

With these cryptic words, the presence disappeared. Kalla drew in a breath of her own, horrified that she had been willing to cold-bloodedly murder someone with her gift, much less drag out the suffering. Grief overwhelmed her. From the shared visions, the Healer had learned more of Dashmari society, and of the War Mage himself, than ever she might have. More than that, she understood how badly she'd hurt him. While she'd been correct in thinking he'd sought her out for her power, the reasons had been all wrong. He'd been willing to relinquish his own power to her, an omega wolf submitting to an alpha in return for protection and acceptance.

The Dashmari didn't just pattern their society after the frost wolves. There was more than a bit of truth in the legends that they were descended from the wolf god Kituk. They *were* frost wolves, given a human form. In a frost wolf pack, Kalla knew, such an odd cub would have been killed outright, and it was so with the Dashmari themselves as well. If, for some reason, the cub survived, their only hope was to attach themselves to a stronger wolf, in the hopes of protection. He had sought her out for that reason, somehow instinctively knowing that part of her soul was frost wolf, even if she hadn't realized it herself. She hadn't know that until she'd seen the Fox King's visions and sought to understand them. He'd recognized a kindred spirit and an alpha at that.

From his memories, too, she realized that the unwanted cub would have been happy with whatever snippets of affection she'd have cared to give, that an unwavering loyalty would have rewarded her mere condescension to accept him. That loyalty had been given to Grosso instead, the only one who had given him the attention and protection he'd craved, no matter how indifferent or impassive. And from Grosso, who must have been serving the Nagali for years, he became infected with Al'dhumarna's taint. It had consumed him, eating away at his heart and soul. She knew now that the Nagali had ordered him to 'dispose of the troublesome mage and her little fox.' He hadn't wanted to, for deep down he still cared for her and sought her approval and acceptance, but the Nagali had a stranglehold on his mind. What he'd done and been a part of had nearly destroyed him. When Grosso had freed him, he'd been half-mad and easy prey for more of the Nagali's evil suggestions.

How much different might his life have been if she'd actually bothered to befriend him as a child rather than merely defending him on occasion. She also knew that Grosso had freed him as a diversion. If he managed to kill Kalla and Aleister, well and good, but it had never been intended that he survive. As the voice had said, he was no longer useful.

A final thought- *why me?*- buzzed through her mind before she relinquished to the darkness seeking to engulf her, falling across the unconscious frost wolf.

Aleister danced back as the mace came swinging forward again. As before, Shingar was extremely blunt and straight-forward. Armoured as he was, the huge magister was well-protected against most weapons. Using the swords would require that Aleister get close enough to the hulking behemoth to slip one between the plates of armour.

Aleister staggered as the mace slammed into a hastily con-jured shield. He'd done his best to avoid Shingar's weapon for as long as he could. He remembered all too well what had happened last time. The shield held and for that he was grateful, but for how long? He ducked another blow and backed away.

From across the courtyard, he heard Kalla taunting the War Mage. Shortly after he felt her shields collapse. The magister panicked, torn between keeping Shingar occupied and helping Kalla. Not that Shingar would matter if she died. The big magister lunged forward again, but stumbled, disoriented. Aleister risked a glance to Kalla and found her on the ground, Vander kneeling before her. Taking advantage of Shingar's inattention, the Sky Fox darted closer. Shingar aimed a clumsy blow at him, but Aleister avoided it easily.

Before the Magister could bring the mace back around, Aleister darted in closer. He plunged one of the slender swords into opening below the armpit, one of the few vulnerable places in the spiky armor. The blade struck true, sliding between the ribs. Shingar crumpled as Aleister backed away. Another glance over to his mage, and he forgot about Shingar in his haste to get to Kalla. The War Mage was gone. In his place lay a great frost wolf, fur the color of summer sunset. Ropes of thin, white-furred scars laced his chest and back. The Healer had collapsed on top of the wolf, but she was still breathing. Even as Aleister reached her, those beyond the warding broke through and, in a flurry of activity, they were quickly surrounded.

Twice the Trouble

Cryshal Kanlon, 10000 ft. above Evalyce, Year of the Mythril Serpent, 2014 CE

Vander slowly came awake and, upon waking, wished he hadn't. He hurt, great Balgeras, how he hurt. His very lungs seemed bruised and sore. Vander blinked gritty eyes. The room slid into focus, an expanse of smooth grey stone, bounded by three stone walls and a wooden door with bars set high up. He was in one of the Kanlon's dungeon cells.

A heavy iron collar was fixed about the frost wolf's neck, a chain leading to the wall. A muzzle pinched his jaws painfully shut and all four paws were shackled together. More than that, his powers were bound again. The wolf was as helpless as a lamb set for slaughter. The ever present presence of Shingar was gone and he guessed that Aleister had managed to slay the big magister after all.

Vander whined softly, fleeting memories of the night before assaulting him. He remembered attacking Hauss, the inferno that had felled the Chief Healer, and wondered if he were still alive. A memory of Kalla's taunting words. The mage's cold expression. The cool voice urging her to go ahead and kill him. The rasping voice that had freed him, changed him. Given him a second chance and made him Kalla's responsibility.

Responsibility. Hah. Kalla's burden and one she most likely wouldn't want to deal with. He whimpered again and tried to curl up, but the chains and shackles made it difficult. He had no idea how long he lay, alone in the dark before he heard voices in the hall. They stopped outside the cell door. A key turned in the lock and the door scraped open. In filed Sevrus sin'Wyvaldor and two maesters bearing a thick pole.

The Sevfahlan mage was dressed in the formal robes of the 'Sin's judiciary capacity. A mane of unruly raven hair framed a face set in hard lines, his sea-green eyes grim. Without a word, the pole-bearers unlocked the collar from the wall and slipped the stout pole through the shackles binding Vander's paws. The frost wolf grunted as they stood, gripping the pole at either end and forcing all of his weight onto his bound paws.

Silently they followed Sevrus down a long corridor, with Vander swinging from the pole like some game hunter's prized trophy, the tail of his mane brushing the floor. He shivered inside, for what a fine trophy a red frost wolf pelt would make! He knew where they were taking him. This corridor had only one termination.

They were taking him to the Hall of Execution.

Apparently Kalla had decided that she didn't want to be burdened with his unwanted presence after all, not that he blamed her in the least. They entered the Hall and Vander saw that others were already there, though Kalla wasn't among them. He recognized Warryn, standing to one side of a long stone table that rose waist high from the ground. The Archivist would be here as witness. To the other side stood one of the Nameless, the executioners of De Sikkari, cowl pulled up to hide his face. The Nameless were all trained magi, their skills and knowledge used to end life rather than save it. In the shadows beyond stood three silent, watchful figures, the magisters belonging to Sevrus, Warryn and the Nameless. The bearers laid Vander on the stone table and withdrew from the room, taking the pole with them.

Sevrus loomed over him, eyes like frozen sea-foam glaring down at the bound wolf.

"Vander kyl'Solidor, you have been found guilty of being a traitor to the Kanlon and a threat to the people. The sentence is death by *sinnis fal,* the execution to be carried out immediately." Sevrus' voice was flat, cold, matter-of-fact.

A thin whimper escaped the wolf at the 'Sin's harsh words. Warryn flicked a sympathetic look towards Vander as he dutifully recorded the judgment. Vander supposed it could be worse. The combined poisons of *sinnis fal* would put him to sleep. His passing would be painless and unlamented.

Vander closed his eyes as the Nameless stepped up to the table and unfurled his equipment. The wolf tried to tell himself that it would all be over soon, but he couldn't keep himself from whimpering. The man gently but efficiently rearranged his paws, seeking the best spot to work. Vander flinched as he felt the needle slide smoothly into his foreleg. A sensation of icy numbness followed it, spreading throughout his body. The first injection. He felt a pressure as the executioner slipped the first needle out and placed the second.

There was a sharp crack of power and an angry presence filled his mind.

"STOP!" A voice full of fury thundered through the room, the person's power crackling through the air, stronger than any he'd ever felt. The scent of rowan filled his nose. The wolf cracked an eye open. Kalla stood before the stone table, the Sky Fox behind her. She looked different and he realized that she now had ears like a Dashmari and a silver frosted mane. Her ears were pricked forward and her mane fluffed in anger. She jerked the needle free.

"Keep him stable!" There was so much authority in the voice that the Nameless obediently took up a place beside her. Vander cringed as he once more felt Kalla's power touch him, but this time, instead of hurting him, she began to break down the poison killing him. The wolf realized too, that the new presence in his mind was Kalla as well. Somehow the two magi had come to share a bond similar to that between a mage and their magister.

Ever so slowly, the numbness receded and Vander's mind began to clear. Finally the Healer sat back. Her face was now drawn and haggard, anger still simmering just below the surface. Behind her the others shifted. They had not interfered, not even Sevrus, but now the Sin' made his presence known.

"Kalla, what is this all about? And when did you wake?" the elder Mage's voice made her turn around. Almost absently, she laid a hand on the frost wolf's head. Vander relished the comforting touch, accidental or not. She touched fist to heart, bowing deeply.

"My apologies, Master sin'Wyvaldor. I woke just now. I... we... somehow Vander has become bound to me as Aleister is bound. I... felt him dying, so I woke and so I came to stop it. Balgeras gave him over to me, when he changed the two of us.

"The King of Cats cleansed him of Al'dhumarna's taint. I couldn't just let him die." Kalla turned back to the frost wolf, lying on the table. She gently undid the clasp to the muzzle. As she slid it off a pink tongue flicked her hand in thanks, but otherwise he remained still, wary of having that anger turned on him.

"Master Sevrus, Solidor's guardian himself gave Vander a second chance. I could have killed him then, but Balgeras commanded me not to. I am also bid tell you... House Solidor no longer has a guardian. Grosso broke the tenets. The King of Cats said the breach must be repaired." Whispers of power and the collar and shackles fell away. The magisters shifted, moving forward upon seeing that the frost wolf was free now.

"I wish we'd had this information earlier. This is not good news, to have lost one of the guardians. This will have to be presented to the Sin' and Kalla I can't say that the vote will not come up as execution again." Sevrus sighed and ran his hand over his face. Kalla responded without turning around.

"Master sin'Wyvaldor, I can't break the Healer's trust, but I can tell you that Vander is no longer a threat. I can also tell you that it is the will of Balgeras that he live and that he be my responsibility. I accept. I understand so much more than I did before. Yes, I can assure you that he will cause no further problems."

"Very well, Kalla. Take him with you for now. I will present this information to the others and what will be, will be." Sevrus paused, looking over her with a gaze almost as critical as a Healer's might be. "You should return to the Healer's Hall, or your quarters. Get some more rest. We will summon you later."

The petite Healer nodded, turning her attention back to the frost wolf. Blue eyes met her green and the wolf whined, low in his throat. He rolled over onto his back, twisting his head around to bare his throat to her.

"*I beg forgiveness, Lady.*" Vander's mindvoice was soft, frightened. He didn't expect to receive it. His thoughts told her that he expected to be punished, and harshly. Kalla thought about saying that there was nothing to forgive, for things were not entirely his fault, but the look on his wolfish face said otherwise. He needed to know where he stood.

"*I forgive you,*" she replied in a gentle tone. Without knowing completely why, Kalla reached down and brushed her hand down his throat, following the line of the large vessels there, acutely aware of the life blood flowing within them.

"*Thank you... Dashkele ti'amaraaq.*" The wolf's tail gave a weak wag and he turned his gaze to the impassive magister standing just behind her. The Arkaddian twitched the slightest of grins, his eyes softening, and the wolf relaxed a bit more.

Kalla reached around and gripped the scruff of his neck at the same instant that Aleister placed a hand on her shoulder. With another crack of power, the three found themselves out of the Hall of Execution and in Kalla's quarters. Vander gaped in wolfish amazement. Few magi could so casually teleport themselves, much less two others, but Kalla didn't seem nearly as fazed by it. The changes wrought by the King of Cats had granted her access to more power than she could draw before. She still looked haggard and tired, but not the least drained by the effort.

"I think we could all do with some food and some sleep," the Healer murmured.

"Here, here." Aleister yawned, flopping down in one of the chairs near the door. The wolf lay down beside the chair and put his head on his paws. Vander found he was far more comfortable in this form, than ever he had been in his other. He watched as Kalla pulled the cord that would call the Solidor servants. She shared a look with Aleister as she walked past the two, into the next room, closing the door behind her.

Kalla stretched as she closed the door to her sleeping quarters. Her body was still very much in need of rest and the energy she'd spent was starting to take its toll, though she was keeping it from her... two... magisters. That was such an odd thought, but already she was becoming used to the twin presences. The two of them felt very different in her mind. Aleister's mind was playful, as always it had been, while Vander's was more subdued, more serious. The frost wolf's thoughts were tinged with worry. He was afraid they were going to try and enforce the execution.

Kalla shook her head, muttering to herself. As she changed into a clean set of baggy pants and tunic her thoughts turned to Hauss. She wanted to go and check on him, but she was fairly certain the Healer was fine. When she'd been woken earlier by the newly forged link, she'd briefly heard the gruff Arkaddian's voice, so she knew he was still alive, and if he was that grumpy, he was doing just fine. A spike of fear shot through Vander's link. The servants had arrived quicker than she had expected. From outside the door came a murmur of voices as Aleister asked the servants if they could bring up something to eat. He was just closing the outer door as she opened the one to her sleeping quarters.

"Lunch will be here shortly, milady," the Sky Fox's lilting voice cut through her musings.

"Is it that late already?" Kalla asked, sinking into one of the comfortable chairs in her outer living chamber. Aleister nodded as he settled back into his own chair.

"Dos mere, Aleister. We should eat and rest while we can. There is no telling when they will summon us." Kalla's voice dripped weariness. Her magick use was catching up to her. Aleister shifted in his seat, glancing down at the dejected frost wolf on the floor beside his chair.

"What happened last night, milady?" he asked softly. The mage started to speak, then paused.

"I'm not entirely sure, Aleister." She shared a glance with the frost wolf.

"*May I?*" she asked, mindvoice gentle. The wolf seemed to shrug his shoulders.

"*You are alpha. He is your second. The memories are now yours to share.*" Even as he thought this, Vander looked away. Kalla could tell he was afraid of facing Aleister's ridicule.

"*Look at me,*" Though her voice was soft, the wolf still flinched as he turned back to her. "*Aleister will not take them lightly, this I promise. However, if you do not wish me to share them, I will not.*"

"*If it will help him understand...*" The wolf fell silent. Kalla reached over to Aleister, gesturing for his hand.

"It will be easier to show you," she said. The Sky Fox glanced down at Vander, before silently giving her his hand, bracing for what he knew would come. The sharing was easier this time, the images flashing through his mind. She shared none of Vander's memories, only her own thoughts. Her sadness, her regret, her greater understanding of both him and his people. The battle, her taunting of the War Mage and her trickery.

Aleister suppressed a shudder at the thought of the cold voice urging her to slaughter a now useless tool. It was followed by the voice of Balgeras. The guardian's warning, his promise and his admonitions. The changes he had wrought. The memories ended with her being jolted awake as the connection flared between her and the dying Vander. Kalla withdrew her mind, letting go of his hand. He knew the rest from there, how he had woken with her and she had taken them both to the Hall of Execution.

As Aleister pondered over all he'd been shown, a soft knock came at the door. Kalla opened it and two servants came in, bearing trays of food. They placed them on the table between the chairs and bowed when she thanked them. There were two small, covered plates on one tray. The other held a much larger covered plate, with an empty bowl upturned atop it. Both contained pitchers of spiced fury wine. Seeing her slightly puzzled look, Aleister laughed softly, a sly glint in his eye. He plucked up the bowl and set it in the floor, pouring part of the fury wine into it. He placed the larger plate in the floor beside the bowl, removing the lid as he did so and revealing large steak, cooked rare.

"Wolf he may be, mage he still is. One definitely needing food!" Aleister said by way of explanation.

Said wolf rolled his eyes up at the Sky Fox and his tail swept the floor once. *"He is kind. More than I have a right to expect. Please thank him for me,"* Vander said, mindvoice tinged with sadness.

"You're quite welcome," Aleister replied cheerfully. Mage and wolf blinked.

"You can hear me, now?" Vander asked. Aleister nodded.

"It is coming slowly, but I can hear you. Feel you too, but it's different than what I share with Kalla."

At this the Vander paused and cast his mind inward. He found he could feel the Sky Fox as well, but as the magister had said, the link between them was different.

"I can sense you as well." The wolf's flame-touched ears drooped. *"I would ask your forgiveness as well, Dashtela, for nearly causing your death."*

"What's in the past, is in the past. I'm still here, so no harm done. But what is it that you called me?" Aleister asked.

"Dashtela? You are Kalla's second. That is the proper title for a second. She is alpha, Dashkele."

"Now that we have the formalities out of the way, can we please eat?" Kalla's voice made both jump. Aleister merely grinned, while Vander favored her with a guilty look. She scowled at both of them and picked up one of the smaller plates.

They passed the meal in a companionable silence, but it was over all too quickly. Aleister called the servants back and they collected the empty dishes. By this point sleep was now tugging at all three and underneath it, the ever present worry about the dreaded summons. As Aleister started to leave, Vander panicked. He looked lost and confused, unsure of where he was supposed to go. The mage could feel that he didn't want to spend what might be the last hours of his life alone again. As he struggled to contain these thoughts, Kalla came to a decision. She would offer him the one thing he'd been denied all of his life- the comfort of a pack, for however brief a time.

"Aleister, shift please." The mage's voice was different. It once more held the forceful, commanding tone she'd used at the Hall. The Sky Fox frowned, puzzled, but slipped into the *kitsune* form without question. Beside the flame-colored frost wolf, the russet fox looked much smaller than he actually was. She strode into the sleeping quarters. They stayed where they were until she stuck her head back through the door.

"Well, come on," Kalla said in an exasperated tone. They looked at her for a moment before the fox warily entered the room. The wolf slunk in after him. She gestured to the bed. "Up. Both of you."

This time they exchanged a look with one another before turning to stare at her. Her mane fluffed in irritation and the fox jumped up, curling in a ball against the far wall. The wolf gave a whine before following the fox. Kalla sighed as she slipped into the bed and pulled blankets back up over her, taking note of where they were. If her reaction truly stemmed from her own wolf origins, then knowing they were nearby should keep her from lashing out in her sleep.

"*Why are we here?*" The voice was Aleister's but the thought was shared by both. Beneath that, she could sense Aleister's uncertainty. He remembered all too well that she'd nearly killed him in her sleep.

"Because Vander has nowhere else to go and I'm not going to make him sleep on the floor. You're here because it wouldn't be very fair to make you leave. I think we all need the comfort at the moment."

She turned emerald eyes on the Sky Fox. "And I know what you're thinking. That shouldn't be a problem since I *do* know you're here."

They seemed to accept that as answer enough, or they weren't willing to question the grumpy mage further. The silence stretched out and Kalla was almost asleep when Vander's soft voice pulled her back.

"*Dashkele... if they... if they decide to carry out the execution, will you do it? Please?*" Fear laced the plea. He didn't want to die, but more than that, he didn't want to die at the hands of a cold, indifferent executioner. The Healer rolled over on her back and patted the covers beside her.

"Come here."

The wolf hesitated for a moment before shifting position. He pressed against her, pinning the blankets down, and she placed a hand on his head, gently scratching behind one ear. He whimpered, leaning against the touch.

"I intend to do my best to keep that from happening."

"But if..."

"If they still rule against you, then yes, I will carry it out myself, if that is what you truly wish," she said.

"It would be much appreciated..." His fear diminished and the wolf was soon asleep as the fox already was. Kalla wasn't long after in drifting off, hand still resting on the wolf's head.

* * *

Kalla woke abruptly, as if a switch had been turned on. Vander was still pressed close beside her, his paws twitching as if he were dreaming. She brushed her hand through his soft fur and he quieted. Kalla noticed that Aleister had moved from his spot against the wall, and was now curled in a tight ball beside the wolf, his brushes covering his muzzle. From the angle of the sun streaming through the windows, Kalla guessed that they had been asleep for several hours. Surely the Sin' would summon them soon.

As if on cue, a knock came at the outer door. Kalla reluctantly climbed out from under the blankets, Vander and Aleister waking at the movement. With a lazy stretch, the fox jumped down, shifting as he did. The wolf's fear spiked again and, almost as an unconscious gesture, the magister offered a comforting touch. The knock came again and Kalla opened the door, revealing Warryn and Shelk. She was surprised that they had sent the Archivist to fetch her. He looked drawn and unhappy.

"Tell me, Warryn." Her voice was low enough that her words didn't reach the two behind her. Warryn only shook his head sadly.

"They're ready for you now. I offered to come... I thought a familiar face might be more welcome," he said in a solemn voice. That alone told her how badly things had gone, for it was so unlike the Archivist to be serious for too long. Her face closed down. Somewhere behind her, the frost wolf whimpered, struggling to control his fear. She went to kneel in front of him, pulling his muzzle up so that he looked at her.

"This will not be," she said. Her voice was controlled calm, but beneath the surface a volcanic pressure was building. "I will not let it."

The wolf whined again and she pulled him closer, wrapping him in a hug. He felt thin and so very frail as he trembled against her. She waited until he'd mastered his thoughts somewhat, then rose smoothly to her feet. From the door Warryn and Shelk watched with shared looks of sympathy. Kalla faced them.

"Lead on, old friend. Let's get this over with." For a moment, the Mage had been tempted to teleport the three of them to the Great Spire, but the thought passed as quickly as it came. She needed all of her strength and power to face the coming battle. They started down the hall, Mage and Magister flanking the frost wolf. They made it all the way to the Solidor courtyard before encountering any problems. Here, unfortunately, a crowd had gathered. Vander pressed against her side as they started through the courtyard, anxiety growing with each step.

They were halfway across when Kalla sensed rather than saw the missile that had been launched at the wolf. The eruption came then, washing over her in a cold fury. From deep within her mind, locks shifted, releasing more power. Time seemed to freeze as she threw a shield around the three of them. The missile, a fist-sized rock, glanced off the shield. Warryn backed away as her power and anger grew. The very air pulsed with it, forcing others to fall back as well. It was an electric sensation, like the high voltage wires of the Artificers' compound, that screamed *danger* to any who could hear.

Her mind swam as new sensations flooded in. She was inundated with a barrage of scents and sounds and it took her a moment to realize that she was sensing things as the Dashmari did, as the frost wolves did. Kalla inhaled and in that breath she found she could differentiate among the people. She could tell who was Arkaddian, who Rang'moori, who was the strongest magi, who the weakest. A moment more and she could tell individuals. Warryn, who smelled of Rang'moori, but more than that, of sunshine and wheat fields. Shelk, who smelled of ocean salt. Aleister, behind her, whose distinctive Arkaddian scent was mixed with the scent of fox and, oddly enough, of cinnamon and frankincense.

Kalla could smell the fear, heavy in the air, almost tangible. The sound of hammering heartbeats rang in her ears, a frantic ruby-colored sound. A low growl trickled from her throat.

"Who challenges me?" Her voice was soft, but forceful. The crowd rippled and parted, allowing another Dashmari to face her. Dogin, one of the senior Alchemists. His mane was fluffed with agitation, but his ears were ambivalent, his head turned slightly to the side. He wasn't sure how to deal with her. Kalla hadn't been born Dashmari, yet now she was, and a powerful alpha at that.

"You protect the traitor. You draw power from him. It is not natural." Dogin's voice died away as Kalla laughed, the sound rich in the air. More locks tumbled in her mind and the laughter became laced with a growling.

"Oh, no. This is all me," said the mage. "But let us set him free and see what happens." She sent the barest whisper of power over Vander, snapping the cords that bound his power. She pushed more power through him, washing away the frost wolf's fear, his anxiety, his lack of confidence. She took it all away and left him stronger than before.

Vander shook himself, mane starting to fluff as he gathered his power back and sent it spilling over into Kalla, but it was as a river feeding into the ocean. He stalked forward, growling. With a silent command, Kalla bid him stop and he came to a halt in front of her, mane fluffed, ears pricked forward. Dogin stumbled backward, fear and wonder both on his face. His ears wilted and he sank to the ground, twisting his head to bare his throat, acknowledging both as the stronger.

"Dashkele ti'amaraaq," Dogin breathed, echoing what Vander had called her earlier. Kalla frowned and turned to Aleister. The magister blinked, a surprised look on his face, and for an instant she saw herself as he did. Her irises had bled into the white of her eyes and they glowed with an emerald fire. More than that, a crescent moon marking had appeared on her forehead, just over the spot where a mage's inner eye lay.

Kalla growled as the crowd parted again, this time revealing two of the Sin'- Sevrus and Malik. The magickal disturbance had been enough to bring them hunting the source. Sevrus approached her, outwardly calm, but beneath the still waters, the Sevfahlan mage's scent of autumn apples was laced with fear. The locks had freed great power. She was now stronger than any of the Sin', even the Grand Maester, and they knew it.

"Kalla, what is this?" Sevrus' voice was low and wary, the voice of one caught face to face with a dangerous animal.

"We were attacked. I do not appreciate being attacked," Kalla responded. "The Sin' ruled to uphold the order of execution, yes." She made it a fact rather than a question and the look in Sevrus' eyes was answer enough.

"It was voted better to make an example of him," Sevrus replied.

"Despite the fact that the guardian of Solidor turned his care over to me? And what of the bond between us, Master Sevrus? What of that? It isn't just the two that are linked. It is all three of us. What if, in executing Vander, you killed Aleister as well? Then *you* would have been the ones carrying out Al'dhumarna's wishes.

"I have told you, he is no longer a threat. Would you punish a knife used to kill someone? No, you would punish the wielder of the knife. Vander was but a tool." Kalla's words were growled out. Even as she spoke, the locks shifted again, sliding back into place. Sevrus visibly relaxed as her power levels began to ebb. As they did, Kalla felt the confidence slowly leak out of the frost wolf. She deliberately left Vander's power free, as a mark of her trust.

"He is considered too dangerous," replied the Sevfahlan.

"Master sin'Wyvaldor, she speaks truly. Vander is no longer a danger to any of us." Kalla and Sevrus turned to Dogin. The Alchemist was still kneeling on the ground. He looked from one to the other, a little uncertainly.

Sevrus gestured towards him.

"Go on."

"He is Dashmari, Master sin'Wyvaldor. He is ... least among the wolves. You would call him an omega. Such wolves seek to find a stronger wolf to protect them. In return they give their unconditional loyalty. It is the same with the Dashmari. Lady Kalla has offered her protection and backed it up. He will do as she says," Dogin replied.

During this speech, the red frost wolf had sunk to the ground. His paws covered his muzzle and his ears drooped. Whatever confidence he had gained when the locks were open, he'd lost when they closed. Shame and unhappiness flooded the link between wolf and mage.

"He is the second strongest War Mage the Kanlon has!" Sevrus' voice was disbelieving.

"Magickal strength has nothing to do with the strength of one's own feelings of self-worth. It has nothing to do with one's personality," Kalla said. She knelt beside the red wolf, brushing her fingers through his fur, seeking to ease his mind. "Master Sevrus, Grosso figured out how to use this to his advantage. It was he who chose Vander's course. Had another earned his loyalty and set a different course, he might well have been among the strongest Healers or the strongest Alchemists." A thought from the wolf caused her to twitch a smile. "Or among the Artificers. My Lord, you have my utmost respect, but in this I will fight.

"Let us leave. A voluntary exile. Neither I nor my magisters will return to the Kanlon. Give us leave and we will depart. I still have a promise to keep to Amaterasu. Correct me if I'm wrong, but none of those the Sin' have sent seeking Xibalba have found entrance, have they?"

Sevrus shook his head and shared another look with Malik. "Kalla kyl'Solidor, you have more forgiveness and understanding than any three people put together." He sighed heavily. "You would be correct. None sent have found entrance. Most never returned and those that did were insane, to put it lightly, mage and magister alike. Cristos was the last who went, several weeks ago. He has not yet returned."

The import of the words was not lost on Kalla. Cristos sin'Aerodor was second only to the Grand Maester. If even he could not find entrance to Xibalba, what hope did she have.

"Nevertheless, I have to try. I intend to keep my promise," Kalla said. Sevrus blinked slowly, taking on the look of one conferring with unseen people. No doubt he was speaking with the other Sin'. Behind him, Malik wore a similar expression. The two shared another silent look before the Sevfahlan spoke again.

"Very well, Kalla. Vander is your responsibility. You are free to leave." His face softened, the traces of a smile appearing. "If you should survive, you will be welcome here once more. Until we should meet again." Sevrus bowed, touching fist to heart in a gesture of respect, then turned and strode off, never once looking back.

Xibalba, 'beyond Sikkari', Year of the Mythril Serpent, 2014 CE

In a vast, gloomy cavern a brooding figure sat on a throne crafted of the interlocking bones of myriad creatures, some of which had not walked the earth in millennia. To all outward appearances the figure looked to be a man, tall, with a flowing mane of silvery hair. Eyes the color of a grey winter sky stared into the distance. Or maybe deep within.

If there had been any others to see, they might have noticed that the figure's countenance changed when looked at side-on, from the corner of the eye. If there had been any to see, they would not have stayed long for they would have found themselves confronted by a terrible apparition, clothed in eldritch light. A great, looming spectral creature, with overlong forelimbs and a head resembling a horse's skull, if ever there was a horse that had sharp teeth. Skeletal wings curled around the body and the eye sockets glowed with a bluish fire. Misty vapor wafted out of the nasal cavern as the being sat lost in thought.

This was Araun, Lord of Living Nightmare and Master of the realm of Xibalba.

For several weeks, mage after mage had attempted to breach the barrier between their world and the lower realm of Xibalba. They had approached places of great power, where the barrier was thinnest and done that which they thought would please the Lord of Living Nightmare, so that they would be allowed access. One had been foolish enough to try and force his way through. Some had made it through the gate, but then there were the guardians to contend with.

None had survived, not intact anyway.

The Lord awaited the one who was coming now. The one in whom he recognized a kindred spirit. If she passed his guardians and passed his test, he would give her what the magi sought, the treasured feather of Ma'at, even though to do so would be to bring about the destruction of one of his own 'children', for Al'dhumarna was a creature crafted of the deepest, darkest fears of humanity.

The foolish humans didn't even realize that it was they who had fostered the Nagali's creation. Araun would not mourn the loss of Al'dhumarna, if the mage and her magisters were successful in their endeavors.

Humans had an overwhelming fear of things they did not understand. It was the god's gift to craft these fears into living nightmares. He gave their guilt, their greed, their envy, and their fear tangible form and allowed them to create their own torment. Many despised the Lord of Living Nightmare for that, for what mortal could comprehend that they brought it upon themselves. And their petty thoughts mattered not one whit to the eldritch creature keeping a silent surveillance over the companions as they traveled.

Xibalba

Kalla stared out the window of the ship, her mind still trying to puzzle out the past several days. As she sat and thought, she idly petted the frost wolf's head. Vander sat wedged between the gunner's and captain's chairs with his head in the mage's lap. The touch was a comfort to both, for it helped Kalla to think and it soothed the wolf's nerves. Grateful to be alive, he still felt guilty because he had been the reason the three had been forced to leave. For two of them, Chryshal had been home for the majority of their lives.

For herself, Kalla had no regrets in her choices. Warryn had been unhappy with her voluntary exile, offering to accompany them. She had gently turned him down, as she had Dogin, the Dashmari Alchemist. That had been a surprise, the Alchemist's offer to travel with them. However, Kalla felt she had more than enough company with not one, but two magisters tied to her. Nor would the *Stymphalian* be pleasant quarters with two more people added. The three of them were pushing the limits as it was.

Kalla *had* been allowed to visit Hauss before they left. The gruff Healer had taken the news in stride, sure that she would be successful and back home where she belonged before long. Hauss had been worked on for the better part of a night and day, but the burns he suffered were gone now. All that was left were a series of scars that dappled the lower left of his face, trailing down his neck and into his collar. His left hand also had burn scars and Kalla guessed that there were a great many more along his left side that she could not see. He wore the scars proudly, as any Arkaddian warrior might. When Vander had shyly approached and offered his apologies the Healer had laughed and thanked the War Mage, for how often does a Healer get the opportunity to earn such? Another example of the Arkaddian ability to take things in stride and find the good in any situation. Surprisingly, Hauss shared Kalla's view of said situation, considering Vander a tool rather than the problem itself. For that, Kalla was silently grateful, for her mentor's opinion still meant a great deal to her.

Her bigger concern was the unexpected upsurge in power. Now that she was aware of them, she could feel the locks blocking that extra power, though she couldn't yet actively shift them. Though her eyes had turned back to normal, she was still graced with the crescent moon marking on her forehead. Her sense of smell and hearing had stayed more sensitized, making her far more conscious of people's moods and true feelings than even her magick did. Had Balgeras given her the power boost? Or merely released the potential already within her?

Then there was the issue of attempting to enter Xibalba. The strongest hotspot was located in Arkaddia, the same spot that the others had tried. Kalla wracked her mind for an answer to the question of traveling to the realm of Xibalba. It should have been a simple thing for any mage to gain entrance. Entry wasn't usually the hard part.

The hard part came after, when confronting the guardians.

Unfortunately, if the Lord of Living Nightmare had sealed the portals, there wouldn't be much she could do. Kalla sighed in frustration. Two days of travel hadn't brought any sudden insights.

Beyond the *Stymphalian's* windows, towering columns of inky black clouds marked the borders of Arkaddia. Even from this distance, Kalla could see the sheets of rain pouring from the unnatural thunderclouds. As the first drops of rain pattered against the ship, a scarlet blur swooped by, leveling out on the mage's side. Amaterasu made a face at the rain, causing Kalla to laugh.

As they flew under the leading edge of the cloudbank, Aleister triggered the ship's shields as Kalla wove a shield around the wyvern. Doing so from this distance was more of a challenge, but she managed to complete it just as lightning forked between the *Stymphalian* and Amaterasu. The wyvern's bellow was swallowed by crashing thunder that shook the ship. The scattered rain turned into a torrential downpour as they crossed the border, causing visibility to drop to near nothing. Aleister flew lower, following Kalla's mental nudges.

The place they sought was not far beyond the Arkaddian border. The closer they could get before landing, the less distance they would need to travel in this horrible weather. The sky growled again, long and loud, as if the clouds themselves were angry at being trapped here. The ship was now close enough to the ground that Kalla could see the destruction wrought by the unnatural rains.

The grass seas were gone, replaced in places by standing lakes of water.

In the near distance, Kalla could just make out a small stand of trees, alone in the vast plains. Another mental nudge and Aleister headed the *Stymphalian* for the cluster of trees. He overflew the grove and circled back, seeking a safe place to land in the marshy grassland. The Sky Fox found what he was looking for and brought the ship to ground with a sigh of relief. Even from inside, they could feel the ship sink into the soft earth. Aleister made a face as Amaterasu landed beside the ship. The wyvern looked less than pleased with the downpour.

Kalla sighed and unbuckled herself. She so did not want to go outside, but if they wanted a decent campsite, she was going to have to go out and provide it. Weaving a shield to keep off the rain, she made her way back to the door. Vander followed and she could tell that he'd woven a similar shield about himself. She let her puzzlement filter to him.

"*I can help. It will make things go faster,*" he said. She twitched a smile and brushed her fingers against his fur as she pressed the panel to open the door. She trudged down the stairs, grimacing as she also sank into the sodden ground. Amaterasu had coiled around the ship, tucking her head up under the front. Kalla turned her attention back to the frost wolf.

"Vander, let's start on opposite sides to walk the circle. Walk it twice, counterclockwise. I'll walk clockwise," she said.

The wolf nodded acknowledgment and the pair took their places. As Kalla walked, she wove a shield to keep out the rains and another to leech the water from the ground. As she passed Vander and crossed into the area he'd already walked, she could sense that the War Mage had also crafted a shield of protection and a warding to keep others away. By the time they were done, the ground was mostly dry, save for the very center of the circle. Aleister had emerged from the *Stymphalian* and, with Amaterasu's help, gotten a campfire started. He now stood at the shield perimeter, gazing sadly out at the flooded landscape. Kalla and Vander joined him.

"The herds will die, if the rains do not stop. The grasslands will turn into a sea in truth," Aleister said. Kalla put a hand to his shoulder in silent support. Arkkadia might not be his home now, but it once had been. She knew the magi had tried to turn the storms away, to dissipate them, but it had all been to no avail. The Nagali's sorcery was more than the magi could confront. Just beyond the shield, she could see the trees and the low mound that marked the 'hotspot', the entrance to Xibalba.

Arkaddia, Evalyce, Year of the Mythril Serpent, 2014 CE

Kalla shrugged off her doubts as she stood. Dinner was over. There was no more putting off their mission, no matter how futile it might seem. The Healer bid Amaterasu to keep watch over the ship, fixing it so that the wyvern could leave the shields to hunt if she wished. Kalla was in no way sure how long they would be gone. If they managed to gain entry, time would flow differently there, as it had for Aleister in Inari's Temple. She had tried to get the two magisters to stay behind as well, but they would not be deterred and so it was that all three set out for the mound in the grove.

Magick saturated the very ground around the mound. Closer, one could see that small rocks lined the sides and top, seemingly in a jumble. Kalla unerringly headed for the right side of the low, oblong mound. Here there was an entrance, framed by flat slabs of rock. The ground around the mound was surprisingly dry, the water kept at bay by the magick. The entrance yawned before them, a darker spot in a darkening dusk. The wolf whined as Kalla conjured magelight and tagged it to the two magisters. She shared his feelings. The Healer didn't want to enter the mound either. The magick surrounding it was not the magick of the Kanlon, nor the magick of Mercurius' children. It was the magick of things far stronger and far older. A cold magick that sent shivers up her spine.

Kalla took a deep breath and plunged through the entryway, magisters trailing behind her. The air within the large chamber was oppressive. The chamber had a broad, smooth floor. Along the walls, paintings of nightmarish creatures danced eerily in the bobbing magelight. Skeletal creatures half dog, half horse, tattered flesh still clinging to bone. A giant wolf with two heads.

A lion-like beast with a man's head and the sting of a scorpion. Carved into the floor was a massive seven circled spiral, flanked by three smaller spirals the size of a man's hand.

The far side of the room, beyond the spirals, was shrouded in darkness still, but twinkles of blue fire winked at them from high up on the wall. Kalla stepped closer and her magelight illuminated the wall, revealing the source. A painting larger than any of the others, of a bizarre creature with oddly proportioned limbs and a head resembling a dog's skull. Skeletal wings spread out from the being, wingtips brushing the far walls. The blue glitter came from sapphires embedded in the creature's empty eye sockets. The painting cast a baleful look over the chamber, as if daring any to come closer.

Swallowing her fear, Kalla walked to the edge of the great spiral. As she studied the carvings and tried to ignore the sapphire gaze of the beast looming over her, the answer came, abrupt and unbidden.

"I know how to gain entry," she said softly. She stepped onto the great spiral, stopping before the small spiral closest to the wall, kneeling to the ground. She gestured to the others to do the same. As they took up places before the other spirals, she withdrew her hidden dagger. "We need to make a blood offering, to fill the grooves of the smaller spirals."

The mage gestured for Vander to give her a paw. He turned uncertain eyes up at her, warily extending a paw and looking away as she drew the sharp blade across his paw pad. Blood welled up from the cut and he held his paw over the small spiral, letting the blood spill into the grooves. When they were full Kalla took his paw and healed it. She repeated the process with Aleister.

Finally it was her turn. She jerked the blade across her palm in a quick gesture, wincing at the sharp pain that followed. She made a fist, letting the blood leak out, onto the last spiral. As the final groove filled in, a soundless concussion of power rocked the chamber, leaving them dazed. They were through. Where the painting had loomed, now a passage extended further on. And yet, the painting was still there. The world beyond overlay the world they had come from.

Kalla rose to her feet, the others doing likewise. She started down the newly opened path. Vander slunk up beside her, ears twitching uncertainly. Aleister moved to her other side, keeping pace with her.

The corridor they followed had smooth, glassy black walls, as if made from obsidian. They followed the corridor for about twenty minutes before they reached a larger chamber. The magelight revealed three smooth walls before them. Kalla snarled, feeling a headache building.

To all appearances they had reached a dead end. As the three of them tumbled out of the corridor and into the chamber a misty light appeared at the far wall. The mist coalesced into a pair of the half dog, half horse creatures. Beside her, Vander growled, mane fluffed.

"*Ghilan,*" he whispered in his companions' minds. Purple fire lit the creatures' empty eye sockets. A low, harsh sound rattled from their throats and it took Kalla moment to realize that they were laughing.

"So. You remember, child of wolves," rasped one of the creatures. "Despite the fact that the King of Cats cleansed you." Another rattling laugh and the being turned its fiery gaze to Kalla. "Mother of Wolves, to pass us you must answer our riddle to our satisfaction."

Kalla nodded. "Very well."

"Jusst sso," the other ghilan hissed. "Tell uss- what is the greatesst of all illusionss?"

"*Time...*" *said* Aleister slowly, remembering his visit to the Temple of Inari, where his week had been a mere two days to Kalla, locked outside. Vander merely shrugged an agreement. His attention was still focused on the ghilan, his mind a flurry of anxiety. She wondered when and why he had met the ghilan before.

"Time," Kalla said, echoing her magister's mindvoice. The ghilan stared at her a moment, weighing the answer. One nodded.

"Correct." It disappeared.

"You may passs," the second said. As it too disappeared back into mist, the wall behind it shimmered and winked out, leaving the passage open. Vander relaxed as the creatures vanished.

The trio followed the newly opened passage for another twenty minutes or so, before reaching a second chamber. This one held the twin-headed wolf from the paintings. As they entered, the giant ink-black wolf rose to its haunches, ears pricked forward. Beyond the wolf, they could see the continuation of the passage. Bones littered the chamber, a mute testament to those foolish enough to try their luck. Kalla could sense that some of the bones had once belonged to magi, explaining what had happened to some of the missing ones. Not all of the bones littering the chamber were human either. Among the scattered remnants, Kalla glimpsed what looked to be a dragon's skull, save that it was far too small. Close to it lay a wickedly curved claw unlike any she was familiar with.

"We are Garm, guardian of Xibalba. We give you this chance. Turn back. Once we ask our question an answer must be given and payment exacted." Amber eyes blinked slowly in the magelight.

"What payment, great Garm?" Kalla asked.

"Answer correctly and you may pass unscathed. Answer incorrectly and you will join the bones of those who came before. No answer is considered a wrong answer. Each of you must answer the same question, according to your own hearts," Garm rumbled.

Kalla shared a look with the others. Vander's ears drooped, and he rubbed his head against her leg for assurance. Aleister merely gave her a mischievous grin. The Sky Fox was by far the more confident of the two. From deep within, the mage felt some of the locks shift, ever so slightly. She stood tall, meeting the guardian's amber gaze.

"Very well, we will answer," Kalla said, low and calm. Garm merely blinked at her again.

"As you will..." the left head sighed.

"What are three things of greatest value in the world, past, present and future?" the other growled.

Kalla pondered the question for a moment. Many answers tumbled through her mind and she discarded them all. Too predictable. She let her mind wander and images flashed past. Warryn and Shelk, hunched over books in the Archives. Hauss, the gruff Arkaddian attempting to teach a young Kalla how to play the thunderdrums. Amaterasu, swooping around the *Stymphalian*. Aleister, just after he'd reappeared from Inari's temple. Vander, lying on the stone table, at the mercy of the Nameless.

"Friendship," Kalla said softly. She wasn't aware that she'd shared the thoughts with the others until she felt Vander press against her leg. To the other side, Aleister placed a comforting hand on her shoulder. The mage lay a hand to the frost wolf's head and with her other covered Aleister's, squeezing it gently.

"*Acceptance.*" The frost wolf's quiet mindvoice carried more confidence than it had before. He now stood alert and calm. Apparently Garm could hear Vander as well because the left head gave a nod.

"A second chance," Aleister's lilting voice followed on the heels of Vander's answer.

Garm lowered his heads, till they were level with Kalla's. She held her ground, fighting the urge to back up.

"Why?" the twin muzzles growled out.

"Because they have no price," three voices chanted back at the giant guardian. They exchanged sheepish looks, when they realized they had spoken at the same time. Garm sat back, seeming to grin.

"Very good. You are free to pass," he rumbled. Kalla bowed to the giant wolf and the three edged by, skirting the cavern along the wall, trying to avoid the gleaming white bones scattered around the chamber. It was with a collective sigh of relief that they slipped through the exit and into the corridor beyond.

More traveling, shunted along in a single direction. Kalla supposed it was a good thing that there were no side passages, that the trip thus far had been straightforward, but Balgeras' teeth it was boring! It seemed as though they had been walking this corridor for ages. Their steps were beginning to drag. Kalla wondered how their time within Xibalba had passed for the wyvern, stuck watching the ship. Kalla felt bad. It seemed that Amaterasu got left behind quite often. The wyvern accepted that there were places she simply could not go because she was so large, but Kalla hoped that trend would change once they left Xibalba.

The bobbing magelights illuminated the approach of another chamber ahead. The trio slowed. After the last two guardians, Kalla was almost afraid of what might be required here. She stepped through, into a chamber like the first, with no exit. A statue stood in the middle of the chamber. As they drew nearer, the statue shifted. Stone cracked and fell away in great chunks, revealing the last of the guardians depicted in the paintings. A manticora, a beast with the body of a lion, the head of a man, and the sting of a scorpion. The creature's deadly tail lashed the ground twice before curling over its back.

"Greetings, mage," the manticora purred. Red eyes fixed themselves on the group. "You have passed the ghilan and you have passed Garm. I am the final guardian. Pass my test and you win your audience with the Lord of Living Nightmare.

"Mage, you and your magisters have made it farther than any in a very long time. Why do you seek to face the Lord so badly?" The manticora's tail twitched again. Kalla frowned.

"We seek the Lord of Living Nightmare because it is he that has the Quill of Ma'at. We need it to recreate the binding of Al'dhumarna," she replied.

The manticora laughed, a deep malicious sound. "What makes you think the Lord would give you the Quill, mage? Mayhap he does not wish the Nagali sealed once more."

Kalla's eyes widened. "Why would the Lord of Xibalba wish the Nagali free?"

"Do you know what it is the Lord of Living Nightmare does, little mage?" the manticora asked.

"He brings the nightmares to us," she relied, voice low.

"No! He merely gives shape and form to the hearts of men. Insatiable greed, bitter envy, burning lust, gnawing guilt. And fear. Fear above all else, for men fear so much. He brings them to life, these dark emotions. The reverse is true as well. He can breathe life into bright emotions just as easily.

"But you do not learn. Humans never learn. You fear and despise the Lord, when it is you who shape your own torment. Al'dhumarna is one such creation." The guardian favored them with a malevolent grin.

Kalla's mind spun with the implications of what the manticora had told them. If it were true, why should the Lord of Xibalba be willing to help them?

"Nevertheless, we must try," she said. "What is your test, that we may pass?"

The sting twitched again, as if the guardian were irritated. "Very well. Answer this and you may pass- What is the mark of true wisdom?"

Thinking of all the manticora had just told them, Kalla met the guardian's gaze and answered without hesitation.

"It is to acknowledge that one knows nothing at all." A whisper through her soul and more of the locks slid open. The two magisters looked to her and from their expressions, she guessed that her eyes had changed once more. Her swirling thoughts stilled, the calm collectedness gathering itself around her once more.

"You may proceed. Let's see if you pass Lord Araun's test intact." The manticora laughed once more and with a flash of light, the guardian was gone, leaving only the stone fragments littering the floor to show that it had been there at all. The light had revealed the exit as well, on the far side of the chamber.

A Question of Ethics

Kalla and her magisters stepped through the doorway and, with a disconcerting sensation, found themselves in a vast chamber lit by a supernatural glow. The only thing in the cavernous room was a throne, crafted of bone. On the throne sat the great being from the painting before the spirals. A dim part of Kalla's mind howled with terror, but she shoved it down. Surprisingly, she felt no upsurge in fear from the two at her side.

"What do you see?" she asked quietly. From across the room, Araun was content to merely wait impassively until they approached.

"I see a man," Aleister replied.

"*I see a man also,*" came Vander's response.

She gave them an incredulous look. "You see a man? Nothing more?"

"No, milady. I see a tall man with long silver-white hair. No more than that," Aleister said. Vander chuffed an agreement and Kalla ran a hand over her face. Why was she the only one who could see the Lord of Xibalba for what he really was? It couldn't be because she was magi for Vander was that also. The only difference between the three was that she was the only female.

Wasn't it? Cautiously the mage approached the throne. As she did so, more of the locks opened and her fear washed away. From the throne, Araun seemed to grin, but then, all skulls seem to grin.

She bowed as she came closer and to her surprise, the Lord of Xibalba bowed back, dipping his head low.

All is One. Araun's voice blew through her mind like a chill wind through autumn leaves. Though he didn't speak aloud, she knew the others had heard him as well.

"One is All,' she responded, then blinked. Where had that come from?

As above

"So below."

"*Thus are all Connected.*" This last she said at the same time as Araun. He nodded slightly, as if satisfied. Kalla was left baffled over the exchange. How had she known the proper responses to the Lord's words?

Greetings, Amaraaq. Welcome to Xibalba. Araun inclined his head towards the others. *And to you, magisters.*

And there was that strange name again, the name Vander had called her.

Few dare to brave the trials of Xibalba, Mother of Wolves. What brings you?

Despite the question, Kalla had the feeling that Araun already knew exactly what she sought.

"We seek the Quill of Ma'at, Lord Araun."

Ahh, the Quill. Indeed. And why should I give it to you, Amaraaq? He shifted on the bone throne, skeletal wings rattling.

"My Lord, I suspect you already know the answer to that. We seek the Quill so that we may recreate the binding that seals Al'dhumarna," she replied.

Of what concern is that to me?

"Because the Nagali is waking. The world is in havoc and he is not yet fully free," Kalla said.

I know. I have no reason to fear the Nagali. Give me one good reason why I should be willing to help humanity.

Kalla faltered. What reason could she give to one who was a god and that, while acknowledged, was not well-liked. A thought chased through her mind, an image of a time when the Lord of Living Nightmare was revered and respected. It was those ancient peoples who had built the mound covering the portal.

"I have no answer to that, my Lord." She knelt before the throne, laying her staff before her. Behind her, the magisters followed her gesture. "I am willing to do whatever you require to obtain that which I seek. I made a promise. I intend to keep it."

Whatever I require… Are you so sure of that, Amaraaq? What if the price of my payment is the lives of the two behind you? Would you be so willing to pay it then?

Kalla felt the kneeling magisters stiffen. A wave of resignation hit her, from both of them.

"*Do it,*" Vander whispered.

"But-"

"*No buts, milady. If our lives can help to save so many others, then do it,*" Aleister said gently. There was a hint of his mischievous smile in the words. "*It's been a pleasure to serve, milady.*"

"That is your price then, my Lord? You wish the lives of my magisters?" Kalla tried to keep her voice even. In the deepest part of her soul, she felt the volcanic pressure building once more. More locks shifted.

If it were, would you be willing to pay it?

"Yes," Kalla growled out the word. Araun snorted, misty vapor issuing from the empty nasal cavity.

That's more like it. No, that is not my price. You may keep your magisters. You will have need of at least one of them very soon. Laughter laced the dry voice. *Indeed. I think you will have a harder time passing Ganysha's requirement to enter his realm. You must make yourself whole, to embrace all that you are in order to access the true depths of your power.*

But that is neither here nor there. You must still meet my price. I wish you to collect one who rightfully belongs to me.

"One who rightfully belongs to you?" she asked.

Yes. He made a bargain with me, if I would take away the nightmares haunting his wife's dreams. They had tried all the more traditional cures and pleas to Azurai, the Dreamwalker.

I did as requested, with the price of payment being a term of service to me, upon his wife's death. If he had bothered to ask, I would have told him that the nightmares were all that were keeping her alive. When I removed them, she killed herself. She would have done eventually, but she would have lived longer as the nightmares were sustaining her in some perverse way only a human could comprehend.

Nor did he want to know why she was suffering from them. My... brother... did not keep them from her for she deserved them. They were dreams borne of guilt, dreams shaped by my gift. The wife had killed their young child, in a fit of pique. The husband thought the death natural and the dreams from stress alone. Not so. I did as I said I would, but the man blamed me for his wife's death and refused to honor his contract. He has managed to gain protection from me by beseeching Azurai's help. My brother granted the man protection because he felt my contract unjust. He believes I should have explained things to the man.

I was merely content to wait until his natural death to claim what is mine, however, it can be the price of your payment. If you were willing to give me those close to you, surely this will be nothing.

Kalla's lips drew back in a snarl and she growled low in her throat. Her mane fluffed and her ears pricked forward, then went flat. The thought of killing a child was anathema to her. She felt sorry for the man, who had lost a family. Yet still, the woman deserved what she had received. And to break a pact with a god was unthinkable.

"I will do it. If we leave, will the guardians allow us passage back in?" she growled out.

It will not be necessary to leave Xibalba in body. You must leave in spirit and so can go where needed. Journeying is not a difficult task for you, Lady Amaraaq. Your magisters will remain here. The Lord of Living Nightmare gestured, conjuring a glass globe, which he then tossed to Kalla. She snatched it out of the air.

This is a soul orb. Draw out his spirit and bring it back with you.

"So he will die?" Kalla asked. Araun snorted again, more mist billowing forth.

He will die. The term of service is for seven hundred years. He knew he would die when his wife did, when he made the pact. I made the terms crystal clear.

"With all due respect, Lord Araun, why would Azurai allow me to do what he denies you?" Kalla growled. The Lord of Living Nightmare threw back his head and laughed, a cold, harsh sound.

By now Azurai knows what is at stake. My brother has more sympathy for the humans than I do. The good of the many and all that. If you can do it, he will not stop you. The question, Mother of Wolves, is: can you? Can you take a healthy life coldly and deliberately?

* * *

Kalla paced the small room Araun had given over to her so that she could carry out her task. The room itself was well-furnished, set in the style of Arkaddia. The mage could only guess at their host's choice of décor. Mayhap because they had entered from Arkaddia?

Kalla stopped her angry pacing and used the cushions and blankets littering the floor to make a comfortable nest in one corner of the room. She settled down, resting her back against the wall. Vander came to lie beside her, head resting in her lap, while Aleister took up a position in the opposite corner. Kalla idly stroked the wolf's fur with one hand. In the other she held the soul orb. The frost wolf's ears swiveled as he listened for anything out of the ordinary, his mannerisms easy and confident, as they seemed to get when the locks on her power were open.

"*Do you wish me to do this, Dashkele? I am not so skilled in journeying as you, but I can do it.*" Vander's thoughts were muted. Kalla felt a flash of guilt and shame and she pulled a strand from his tangled thoughts before he could push the memories away. He was heartsick at the thought that one who was a Healer must be made to carry out such a ruthless task, when it was one better given to a person whose soul was already tainted with such ruthlessness.

"No, Vander. I must do this. I would not use you as Grosso did. I thank you for the offer," she said gently.

"*Are you sure, Dahskele? I do not mind. I would save you from this pain, if you would let me.*"

"I am sure." She gathered her strength about her. Better to carry out this task while the locks were still open. She had no control over them, thus no idea how long she could rely on the added strength.

The mage sighed. It was no use putting this off any longer. Though journeying was best accomplished by slow relaxation, she used her newfound strength to speed up the process, willing her spirit back into the world 'beyond', where they had come from. With the vertiginous sensation that usually accompanied such transitions, Kalla found herself back in the chamber of the Spiral. Araun had placed in her mind the necessary information to locate the man in question. It was merely a matter of thought to travel to where she needed to go.

Her spirit drifted, smoke on the wind, seeking out her target. She was in Inkanata, the continent to the east of Evalyce. A sere wind blew through desert dunes, though she could not feel it. Before her lay a city of tents surrounding an oasis, home of the desert nomads. This was a place far removed from anything she'd ever known. Though the Healer had traveled the length and breadth of Evalyce, she had never crossed the Aeryth Ocean to Ishkar, nor the Tezac Ocean to visit the Ramerides. What she knew of these lands came from the magi at the Kanlon who had come from them. Malik sin'Solidor was one such, hailing from Ishkar, in Inkanata.

The tents were dark shapes in the night, billowing forms that swayed with the unnaturally hot wind. A line of long-necked pack animals stood nearby. As the mage glided past, they snorted, stamping softly. Though they could not see her, the animals could sense her and the unseen presence made them nervous. She followed the trace of her target until she came to a small, shabby tent on the far side of the encampment. Clearly her intended victim had fallen on hard times.

Kalla flitted through the tent flap, entering into a small, cramped living space. A man slept fitfully on a pallet in the floor. As she entered, the man's eyes flew open. He drew in a long, ragged breath.

"Who's there?" he whispered fearfully. The mage steeled herself and willed her body into a misty visibility, causing the man to gasp and shrink away, too terrified to even scream.

"Who are you? What do you want?" he whimpered faintly.

"I am Lady Kalla. I've come to collect on your contract with the Lord of Living Nightmare," she said softly. The man whimpered again.

"No…"

"I am sorry. However, you made the deal. It isn't a wise choice to renege on a deal with a god," Kalla said.

"He caused her death!" the man exclaimed forcefully.

"Not so. The nightmares were all that were keeping her alive. If you'd left well enough alone, she would have lived longer. Either way, suicide would have been her choice. The dreams were borne of a guilty conscience," the Mage replied.

"That's not true!"

"Yes. It is." Kalla sighed. "You should have asked Lord Araun 'why' your wife was suffering from nightmares that not even Azurai would banish. He would have answered.

"Your wife killed your son on purpose. She was angry with a child being... well... a child. The nightmares were her guilt made manifest."

The man shook his head. "That can't be..."

"Nevertheless, that it is and now you must fulfill your end of the contract." Kalla looked around the shabby tent sadly. "And would that really be such a bad thing?"

"Why are you doing the dirty work?" the man asked.

"Because you have Azurai's protection against Araun himself. Unfortunately for you, the Dreamwalker must have more of a reason to let me carry out the task than to extend the protection to include me. This is the job Araun gave me to do in return for something I am in great need of," Kalla replied.

"I don't want to die..."

"I am sorry," the mage said softly. She drifted forward, causing the man to cringe away. Stretching out her hand, she rested her phantom fingertips against the man's forehead. Using the same tactic as when she journeyed, she gently began to draw his spirit out of his physical body. The man wailed, his body thrashing like a fish on a hook and Kalla almost gave up. Her soul cried with him, but she grimly stuck with her task. This was Araun's price. If she didn't do it, then they would not get the Quill and their quest would be lost before it had really begun. Finally, the body stilled, as most of the animating force was now gone from it.

As soon as the man's spirit was completely free, she pulled the both of them back to her own body. She came to herself with a gasp. The soul orb in her hand glowed brightly and the mage shuddered at the thought of what she'd been forced to do.

"*Dashkele, are you alright?*" Vander asked quietly.

"I'm fine. How long was I out?"

"It's been about two hours," Aleister replied. Worry tinged his words and thoughts as he sensed her inner turmoil. Seeing her struggling to rise, he offered a hand and pulled her up. Araun had said to simply announce when they were done and they would be guided back to the throne room.

"Lord Araun, I have finished. I have done as you commanded," she announced to the room in general. With a rasping laughter, two ghilan appeared before them. The spectral creatures eyed the glowing orb and nodded in satisfaction.

"Very well. Follow usss," one sighed, in its strange, rasping voice. Kalla gave a curt nod and the ghilan trotted off, mage and magisters following behind. They crossed the door threshold and found themselves once more in the throne room.

As Kalla approached the Lord of Living Nightmare, the locks began to shift closed. *Not now!* she thought desperately. They had sustained her far longer than she expected, but she wished that the locks would stay open until she were out of Xibalba. Araun's skeletal wings rustled as they neared.

Well, Lady Amaraaq. It seems you managed to carry out the task after all. Mist wafted from the nasal cavern as he deftly caught the orb that she threw to him.

"Yes, my Lord," she growled out. Araun merely laughed, in that winter wind voice.

You have done well, Mother of Wolves. He held the glass orb before him, drawing the man's spirit from within. For a moment the man looked disoriented. Then he saw where he was and dropped to his knees with a terrified wail that cut Kalla to her very core. As more locks whispered shut an altogether different kind of pressure began to build. Self-loathing. Horror at what she'd done. She tried to hide the thoughts from her magisters, using the remaining locks as a buffer.

On the throne, Araun regarded his victim impassively. He leaned forward, coming closer and the man wailed in terror again.

Forget. The Lord snorted, blowing a thick mist over the man. As it touched him, the man shifted and changed, taking on the more solid form of a slender white hound with red ears. He would serve his term as one of the Coinn Iotair, one of the Wild Hunt. The hound settled on the floor before the throne, clearly no longer afraid.

See, I am not so heartless as you think me. He will remember nothing. When his time is up, his soul will be free to make the same choices as any other. Araun made another gesture, conjuring a cylindrical leather case. He held it in his hands a moment before undoing the clasps. Gingerly he drew out a white plume, some two feet long. It glowed gently, a luminescence held within. *The Quill of Ma'at. Your price.* He slipped the feather gently back into its case and tossed it to Kalla. She slipped the strap over her shoulder so that the case rested against her back.

"Thank you, Lord Araun." Kalla bowed low to the Lord of Living Nightmare.

You are welcome, Lady Amaraaq. May your journey be successful. Another flick and a whistle fell out of the air, closer to Kalla. She reached out and caught it, a puzzled look on her face.

"I don't understand, my Lord. What need do I have of a whistle?" she asked.

This a gift I give you freely. It is a magic whistle that can call the Coinn Iotair to you. It will work twice before the magic is gone, so choose wisely, Mother of Wolves.

I will also pass this information on to you for free. You have the Quill, impressive in itself, but in order to reach Ganysha's realm, you must attain your second transition. You must be Lady of Wolves or Laeksheen and Ganysha will not let you pass.

By accepting the bond Balgeras gave you over Vander, you attained Mother of Wolves, your first transition. You are awakening Divinity, little Wolf and you must claim all of your aspects.

"And how do I claim that aspect, Lord Araun?" she whispered as the final locks slid closed.

That depends upon you. Go now, through the door you entered first. It will take you straight back to the portal chamber. Inaba Kaze. Vander kyl'Solidor. Protect her and keep her safe.

Araun's words caused Aleister to freeze for a moment. *Inaba Kaze.* It was a name he'd thought he'd rid himself of long ago. He bowed, turning just in time to catch Kalla as she sank to the ground, whimpering softly.

"What's wrong with her!" Aleister looked to the Lord of Living Nightmare for guidance.

The locks on her Divine power have closed again. They sustained her through her task. Now we see how it really affected her. You must take care of her. If she be as strong as she seems, it will pass quickly enough. If not...

Aleister nodded and scooped up the now sobbing mage. He scooped up the staff as well. Kalla seemed to be trapped in her own mind, for nothing Aleister whispered to her had any kind of reaction. With a last glance back at the Lord of Living Nightmare, Aleister plunged through the door, Vander on his heels. As Araun promised, they were back in the main chamber of the mound. With another soundless concussion of power, the gate closed, leaving them in the 'normal' world. The magister waited while Vander wove shields around them to keep off the rain, then stumbled out of the mound, still carrying the mage. Kalla was quieter now, but she wouldn't respond to anything he said and her eyes had a glassy look to them.

Back within the safety of the ship's shields, Aleister gently lay the mage down on the ground. As he withdrew his touch, she gave a strangled cry that turned back into more sobs. Both he and Vander tried to get a coherent response from her, but Kalla remained locked in her own mind.

"What are we going to do?" Aleister asked Vander. The wolf whined and lay his ears back.

"*Dashtela, ideally we would call a Healer. She has gone deep inside to hide and we may not be able to draw her out again. She may stay locked in her grief. I don't believe that will be the case, nevertheless it may hours or even days before she comes out of it.*"

Aleister sighed. Kalla was the Healer among them and she quite obviously couldn't heal herself. He was more than a little worried. To his senses, her mind felt as if she was asleep. Was it possible for certain areas of a person's mind to shut down in the face of something they couldn't handle. But she seemed so strong... Why would this have made such a difference? Yet, he had that answer too. She'd been forced to take a life 'in cold blood' and he was fairly certain that it was something she'd never done before. Help the dying, yes. Kill the healthy living, no. The Sky Fox wondered if she would have reacted the same way if she'd succeeded in killing Vander, even if it had been in a fight. How he wished Hauss were here! If she didn't get better soon, he would take her back to the Kanlon for help, consequences be damned.

Amaterasu dipped her head down, nudging the Healer gently. She fixed the Sky Fox with a piercing gaze. For the first time since they had met, the wyvern spoke to Aleister.

She is strong. She will be fine. There is more to the Lady than meets the eye.

Aleister smiled and patted the wyvern gently on the muzzle. "I certainly hope so, Lady Amaterasu."

While Vander and Amaterasu watched over her, Aleister brought out blankets from the ship. He tried to take the case containing the Quill from her, to put in the ship, but she refused to give it up. He almost brought food out too, but he was exhausted. From the way Vander was swaying ever so slightly,

Aleister guessed that the wolf was more tired than hungry as well. He joined the wolf and dragon at the Kalla's side and gently covered her with a blanket. She was now lying down, clutching the case as if it were a life preserver, still sobbing softly. Aleister gently brushed his fingers through her hair, making soft shushing noises. To his surprise, she quieted immediately. He drew away and she started sobbing again. He resumed and she quieted once more.

"Why is it only with me? She wasn't this quiet with either of you." the magister asked.

"*Maybe some part of her can still recognize that you mean safety. Despite my bond with her, you are the one she relies on to keep her safe,*" Vander replied.

Aleister sighed and stretched out on the ground beside his mage. He gently pulled her closer to him, keeping an arm wrapped around her. The fact that she didn't object said quite a bit about her mental health. He prayed that she wouldn't be too offended when she came to her senses, but so long as the Sky Fox kept contact with her, she was quiet and still and that was all that mattered to him. Vander's blue eyes met his and Aleister could see they were filled with a mute worry. The frost wolf curled up on the other side of her and, almost as an afterthought, she reached out and pulled him closer, as if he were a giant teddy bear. Vander grunted as the case dug into his side, but didn't fight her. Amaterasu coiled around all three, covering them with a gauzy wing for added warmth.

Alert! Alert!

Heh.... I'm so mean.

This book was never intended to be broken down, so instead I have set it up as a serial, rather than sequels. The entire thing is finished, and the remaining parts should be out in quick succession. Be sure to visit the links provided at the beginning for updates on new works in progress and the status of releases.

I do hope you enjoyed this brief foray into the realm of De Sikkari.

By all means, feel free to contact me:

Twitter: @cala_gobraith

Mail: belsuutcala@gmail.com include Sikkari in the title or it might be binned as spam.